T0166425

&*Isobel*
Emile

Alan Reed

Coach House Books

Toronto

first edition

 Canada Council Conseil des Arts
for the Arts du Canada    ONTARIO ARTS COUNCIL
CONSEIL DES ARTS DE L'ONTARIO   Canadä

Published with the generous assistance of the Canada Council for the
Arts and the Ontario Arts Council. Coach House Books also acknowl-
edges the support of the Government of Canada through the Book
Publishing Industry Development Program and the Government of
Ontario through the Ontario Book Publishing Tax Credit.

The author gratefully acknowledges the financial support of the Alberta
Foundation for the Arts.

LIBRARY AND ARCHIVES CANADA CATALOGUING IN PUBLICATION

Reed, Alan, 1978-
    Isobel and Emile / Alan Reed.

ISBN 978-1-55245-227-1

    I. Title.

PS8635.E35186 2010   C813'.6   C2010-901663-7

'How much less than dreams
are the things we actually do!'
— Paul Poissel

They are sitting.

There are two of them. They are sitting beside each other. They are in a room.

There is a bed in the room. There is a sink. There is a window. There is a door. There are things scattered on the floor and there is an empty bottle under the bed.

They are sitting on the bed. It is a small bed. It has plain white sheets on it. Before they sat on the bed they slept in the bed. They lay together with their arms around each other and their legs together. It was quiet in the room.

They slept.

When they woke up they did not get out of the bed. They stayed the way they had been lying when they were asleep.

They were not wearing clothes. They were naked. They had been naked when they went to bed the night before. It had not troubled them then. It had been dark.

There was light coming in through the window when they woke up. It was early in the morning.

There were specks of dust floating in the light.

They got out of the bed. They did not look at each other. They got out of the bed and they looked for their clothes on the floor.

They had to look for their clothes because they did not know where their clothes were. They knew that they were on the floor. The night before they had taken off their clothes and they had thrown them onto the floor. They did not look where they had thrown them.

They did not care what happened to them then. They wanted them off their bodies. Now they had to look for them.

They found their clothes. They put their clothes on. They looked at each other with their clothes on. They still looked naked. It was their eyes. They were too tender.

They looked at each other and then they looked at themselves standing in the room.

There was nothing else in the room. There were things in the room but they did not matter anymore. They were nothing.

There was nothing else in the room and there was nothing left to do.

They were standing beside the bed. They were wearing their clothes. They did not say anything. There was nothing to say so they did not say anything.

They sat on the bed. There was nothing else to do. They sat beside each other on the small bed with plain white sheets.

It is still quiet in the room. They are sitting beside each other on the bed. It is early in the morning.

They are not sitting on the bed anymore. It is still early in the morning. There is still light coming in through the window.

One of them is standing beside the bed. He says: 'We should go.'

The other one of them is not standing. She is still sitting on the bed. She does not say anything.

She pulls her hands through her hair. She is trying to make her hair lie the way that it is supposed to. Her hair is not lying the way that it is supposed to.

She pulls on it.

If her hair would lie like it is supposed to then something would be different.

She is sure that something would be different. She makes her hands into fists. She pulls on her hair. Tears come to her eyes. It does not matter. Her hair will not lie like it is supposed to. Her hair does not lie like it is supposed to when she has slept on it.

He says: 'We should go.' She closes her eyes.

She nods her head.

There is a suitcase by the door. On top of the suitcase there is a knapsack.

He goes over to where the knapsack is on top of the suitcase. He picks the knapsack up. He puts it on his back. She is sitting on the bed. He bends over to pick the suitcase up.

She looks at him standing by the door. He looks like he does not know how to stand with a suitcase in his hand and a knapsack on his back. He holds them awkwardly.

He says: 'We should go.' He does not say it like he is sure they should go.

She nods her head.

She stands up. She stands in front of the bed for a moment. She pulls at her hair again. It is still not lying like it is supposed to. It does not matter anymore.

He opens the door. She puts her shoes on.

There are stairs on the other side of the door. They are stairs going down.

She goes through the door and she starts to walk down the stairs. The steps are made of wood. Her shoes makes sounds when she steps on them.

After she goes through the door he goes through the door. He closes it behind him. He follows her down the stairs.

In the room they have left there is still light coming in through the window.

There are specks of dust floating in it.

They are outside now. It is brighter here than it was inside. They have to squint their eyes.

They are standing on a street.

It is the main street of a town. There are shops along it. They are not open yet. It is too early in the morning. There is still a chill in the air.

They are going to the train station. They walk down the street and then they turn onto another street. There are no shops on this street. There are row houses built along it. They walk down this street and then they walk out of the town.

Outside the town there are fields. There are fences around the fields. There is nothing left in them. They have been harvested. They are bare now. The light is brighter here. There are no buildings to shade them from it. The light feels like it is pressing down on them.

The train station is here. It is in a field.

The train station looks like a barn. It might have been a barn once but it is not a barn now. Now it is the train station. There is a sign over the door that says that it is the train station.

The train station is painted white. The letters on the sign are painted green.

They walk down the road that leads to the train station. It is getting warmer. They are starting to sweat. They walk and then they are standing in front of the train station.

There is a door that goes into the train station. There is a woman there. She is in a booth. She sells tickets to the people who come into the train station. There are no people in the station to sell tickets to. She is knitting a sweater instead.

They go inside the station.

They go to where the woman is knitting a sweater. He puts his suitcase down. He reaches into his pocket. He takes a piece of paper out. It is a ticket for the train. He shows it to the woman. He asks where he should go to catch the train that is written on the ticket.

The woman there tells him to go to the first platform. She points with her finger. She is sitting on a chair behind a pane of glass. She is very fat.

He picks the suitcase up. They walk to where the woman pointed. There is a door there. It is propped open. On the other side of the door there are the platforms the trains stop at.

There are two platforms. One is for the trains going one way and the other is for the trains going the other way. They go to one of the platforms.

There is a bench on the platform. There is also a bench on the other platform. There is no one sitting on either of the benches. There is no one else here.

It is still early in the morning.

They sit on the bench. They sit so that they are beside each other. They do not say anything. They look at each other and then they look at the bench on the other platform.

There should be something to say. They want there to be something to say.

They cannot think of anything to say.

It scares them.

One of them says: 'I am hungry.' It is not much of something to say. It is stupid. But it is something.

The other one says: 'We should get something to eat.'

They stand up. They go inside the station. There is a snack machine there.

When they go inside the station the woman stops knitting. She watches them.

She watches them as they go over to the snack machine. They stand in front of the snack machine. The snack machine makes a humming sound. There is an electrical motor inside it.

They put coins into the snack machine. Gears inside the machine turn. The snack machine gives them snacks.

The woman inside the station is still watching them. They can feel her watching them. They take their snacks and they go back to the platform.

They were the only people on the platform. Now they are not the only people on the platform. There is another person here.

The other person is wearing a suit and carrying a briefcase. He is carrying his briefcase in his hand. He has taken the jacket of his suit off. It is getting warmer. He is holding the jacket in his other hand.

The man wearing a suit is not sitting on the bench. He is standing near the edge of the platform.

They sit on the bench. They have their snacks. The snacks are wrapped in brown paper. They take the paper off their snacks. They start to eat their snacks.

The man on the platform does not look at them. They are relieved that he does not look at them. He puts his briefcase down. He takes a handkerchief out of his pocket. He wipes his forehead with his handkerchief.

It is going to be a warm day. It will not be warm for much longer. The days are starting to get shorter.

They eat their snacks. They look at each other while they eat. They try to smile.

They do not smile.

They look at their snacks instead. They concentrate on eating.

They concentrate on eating their snacks and then they finish eating their snacks. They are sitting on the bench. They are beside each other. There is a slight breeze. They hold the wrappers their snacks were in. They do not want them to blow away.

They have not thought of anything to say. They know what is happening. They know what is going to happen. They do not need to say anything. There is nothing they can do about it. All they can do is wait for it to happen.

They hold the wrappers their snacks came in. They do not say anything.

They wait.

The man on the platform puts his handkerchief back into his pocket. He does not pick up his briefcase. He pushes up his sleeve to look at his watch. He bends over to pick up his briefcase.

They are sitting on the bench. They do not want to wait for what happens next. They want to do something. They want to say something.

They try to say something.

What they say is not what they want to say to each other. It is almost what they wanted to say to each other but it is not it.

It does not matter. It would not have changed anything.

The train is here.

He stands up. He puts his knapsack on his back. His knapsack had not been on his back. It had been on the bench beside him.

He bends over. He picks his suitcase up. She watches him put his knapsack on his back and then bend over to pick his suitcase up.

She is still sitting on the bench. She is holding her hands together in her lap. The train stops at the platform. She stands up. He is standing near the train. She walks towards him. She stands in front of him. She stands close to him.

She kisses him.

The station attendant opens the doors to the train. There are people on the train waiting to get off. The doors open. The people step off the train. They stand on the platform and then they walk across it. They go into the station.

They do not care that there are people getting off the train. They stand in the middle of the platform. They are young. They are kissing.

The station attendant blows a whistle. It means that the train is going to leave.

He is holding his suitcase in his hand. He steps away from her. He gets on the train.

The station attendant walks down the platform. He closes the doors to the train. She stands on the platform. She watches as the station attendant closes the doors to the train.

The station attendant blows his whistle again.

The train starts to move. She watches as the train starts to move. The train moves slowly and then it moves faster. It pulls away from the station. He is on the train. She is not on the train.

The train pulls away from the station and then it is gone.

She watches it go.

Emile is in a city. He is walking down a street. There are street-cars on the street. There are people walking by him. They are wearing long coats and they have hats on their heads. They brush against him. They do not stop walking. They brush against him and they keep walking.

He is smaller here. He is walking down a street.

In his hand he is carrying a suitcase and he is wearing a knapsack on his back. There are shops along the street. There are restaurants and bars and shops that sell clothes. It is late. The shops that sell clothes are all closed. The people who are walking by him are coming out of the restaurants and bars and going into other restaurants and bars.

He stops. He is standing in front of a bar. The people walking by him do not stop. Someone bumps into him. Emile goes into the bar.

There are people in the bar. They are drinking. There are not many people in the bar. It is not a night for people to go out to bars. But there are some people in the bar. There are people sitting at the tables and there is someone sitting at the bar. There is music playing.

Emile stands in the door. He looks at the people in the bar. They are drinking. He looks at each of them and then he looks away.

He goes to the bar. He sits on a stool. There are stools in front of the bar. He puts his suitcase down beside him. He takes his knapsack off. He puts it on the stool next to him.

A bartender comes over to where Emile is sitting. The bartender stands in front of Emile. He puts his hands on the bar. He looks at Emile.

Emile says: 'Gin and tonic, please.'

The bartender nods his head. He walks away. He comes back with a glass. He puts the glass on the bar in front of Emile.

Emile takes some money out of his pocket. He puts it on the bar. The bartender takes the money. He walks away from Emile.

Emile sips at his drink. He looks around the bar again. He says: 'Excuse me.' He says it again. He says: 'Excuse me.' The bartender comes back. The bartender says: 'Everything all right?'

Emile says: 'Yes.' The bartender is about to walk away again. Emile says: 'Is Nicolas here?'

The bartender says: 'No, he hasn't started yet.' He looks at his watch. He says: 'He'll be here soon.'

Emile says: 'Thank you.'

He picks up his glass. He sips at it. He puts it down on the bar. He waits.

There is a straw in Emile's gin and tonic. It is pressed up against the side of the glass. The ice in the drink is holding it there.

He touches the straw with his finger. It moves slightly.

He touches his finger against the straw again. It moves again. It does not move as much. It does not move as much because the ice does not move. He presses harder. The straw does not move. He wants the straw to move. It is frustrating.

Emile presses against the straw so that it moves around the ice. The ice moves. The straw moves forward. It does not move forward very far.

He was away from the city. Now he is back in the city. He walked down the street to get here. He did not remember what it was like to walk down the street here.

He needs to make sense of it. He is going to make the straw move to the other side of the glass. It will help him to make sense of it.

He is bent over his glass. He is concentrating. The door to the bar opens. Nicolas comes into the bar. Emile does not hear the door open. He is bent over his glass.

Nicolas moves easily. He looks older than Emile. He looks more confident.

Nicolas says: 'Emile?'

Emile's head jerks up. He is very young. He turns around on his stool. He looks around the bar. He sees Nicolas. Nicolas is wearing a fancy scarf. He wears it like he is very pleased that it is a fancy scarf.

Emile says: 'Nicolas.'

He stands up slowly. He is smaller than Nicolas. He does not stand as straight. Nicolas walks over to where Emile is. He opens his arms. He hugs Emile.

Nicolas says: 'It's good to see you.'

Emile says: 'It is good to see you too.'

Nicolas works at the bar.

He is not wearing his scarf anymore. He has an apron tied around his waist. He is standing behind the bar. Emile is sitting on a stool across from him. Emile is drinking another gin and tonic.

Emile says: 'I was on the train all day.'

It is dark outside. The street lights have come on. It is late now. In the morning Emile got on a train.

He stood on the platform of a train station. The train pulled into the station. It stopped. The station attendant walked down the platform. He opened the doors to the train.

There were people who got off the train. After they got off the train Emile got on the train.

He had his suitcase and his knapsack with him. He went up the steps and into the train. There were seats there. There were people sitting in some of the seats and some of the seats were empty.

Emile took off his knapsack. There was a rack over the seats. It was where people were supposed to put their luggage. He put his knapsack on the rack above the seats. It was with other people's luggage. Some of the other people had knapsacks for luggage and some of them had suitcases.

Emile did not put his suitcase on the rack above the seats. He sat down in the seat under his knapsack.

He tried to put his suitcase under the seat in front of him. It did not fit. He put his suitcase under his seat instead. He did not like having his suitcase under his seat. He took his suitcase out from under his seat. He put it on his lap. He held it with his hands.

The cushion on his seat was red. All the seats had red cushions on them and the walls of the train were painted brown. He was sitting next to a window.

He looked out the window. The train was still beside the platform. It had not yet moved. He sat in his seat next to the window and he looked out at the platform.

There had been a girl standing on the platform.

The train started to move. It was moving along the platform and then the platform was gone. Where the platform had been there were things moving past the window. First there were the fields by the station and then there were other fields. The train stopped at a town and then it went past more fields.

There were sheep in the fields. They did not look up at the train. They ate grass instead.

Emile did not look at the sheep.

The train went past another town. There was a station at this town. The train did not stop. The train went through the station and then there were not as many fields. There were buildings where there used to be fields.

The buildings were small and old. Some of them were abandoned. Then the buildings were larger and not as old.

Emile did not look at the buildings. He looked out the window but he did not look at the buildings.

The buildings got larger. They came closer to the tracks. The train kept moving. The buildings were up against the tracks. The train kept moving. There were buildings up against the tracks and then there was a building in front of the tracks. The tracks went into it.

The building in front of the tracks was a station. The train had gone through other stations. It had stopped at some of those stations. Those stations had been platforms built beside the tracks. People waited on the platforms for the train to come.

Those stations were not like this station. This station was larger. The train went inside it. There was a ceiling high up overhead. The ceiling was made of panes of glass. There were pigeons living under it. It was filthy.

Emile looked out the window. He was not looking at anything on the other side of the window. He did not want to look at anything.

He was in the city again.

The train was not the only train in the station. There were other trains here. They were moving. Some of the trains were moving into the station and other trains were moving out of the station.

The train Emile was on went into the station. It stopped. It waited. Emile looked away from the window. He held on to his suitcase. The train waited and then it moved towards a platform.

The train stopped. Emile stood up. He took his knapsack from the rack over his seat. He had his suitcase in his hand.

He tried to get off the train. He could not get off the train. There were people in the way. They were the people who had gotten on the train while Emile was looking out the window. He had not seen them getting on the train. He had been looking out the window.

There were too many people on the train.

Everyone was trying to get off the train. They all moved slowly towards the doors. There were too many people to move quickly. Emile was in the middle of them. They all moved slowly.

They got off the train and they were standing on the platform inside the station. The light coming through the glass ceiling was muted and dirty. They walked off the platform and into the station.

Emile went with them. He had no choice. There were too many of them.

There were more people in the station.

There were people from other trains walking into the station. There were people in the station walking out towards the platforms. They ran up against each other. Emile thought they would slow down. They did not slow down. They sped up.

Emile had forgotten how people walked in the city. It was hard to keep up. The people around him were walking faster. He had to keep up. He walked out of the station and into the street with all the other people walking out of the station and into the street.

Emile was in the street. He had to catch a streetcar.

Emile walked into the street. He went to the place where the streetcars stopped. He waited. He stood with his knapsack on and his suitcase in his hand.

It did not take long for a streetcar to come.

Emile got onto the streetcar. He stopped in front of the fare machine. The fare machine was at the front of the streetcar. It was beside the driver. He put some coins into the fare machine. The driver of the streetcar gave him a ticket.

He went to sit down. There was nowhere to sit down. He put his suitcase between his feet. He held on to the handrail over his head. He tried to look out the windows.

He was looking for the street with the bar on it.

Nicolas puts a stool upside down on top of the bar. Then he puts another stool upside down on top of the bar. He puts stools upside down on top of the bar until all the stools are upside down on top of the bar.

The chairs by the tables are already upside down on top of the tables.

Someone else is mopping the floor. It is the bartender who made Emile's first gin and tonic. They are the only people in the bar.

The bar is closed.

Emile is standing outside the bar. He has his knapsack on his back. His suitcase is on the ground beside him. He is rolling a cigarette.

Nicolas is doing the things that need to be done to close the bar. When he has done the things he needs to do he says good night to the other bartender. He comes out onto the street. He is wearing his fancy scarf again. He locks the door behind him.

Emile hears the door open. He looks up from his cigarette.

Emile says: 'Are you done?'

Nicolas nods his head. He puts the key to the bar in his pocket.

It is starting to get cold at night. Emile wishes he had a scarf with him. He has his collar turned up.

Emile lights his cigarette. He passes it to Nicolas. Nicolas starts to walk away from the bar. Emile picks his suitcase up. He walks away from the bar with Nicolas.

They walk to the next block. It is where the streetcar stops. It is where Emile got off the streetcar on his way here. They go to the platform in the middle of the street. They wait for a streetcar to come.

They pass the cigarette back and forth between them.

A streetcar comes. It stops in front of them. They get on it and they put their fares into the fare machine. The driver gives them tickets. They sit down on the streetcar and the streetcar moves again. They sit on the streetcar for a while. Then they get off.

They are standing on a platform in the middle of another street. There are shops on this street. They go to a door between two of the shops.

Nicolas puts his hand into his pocket. He takes some keys out. He opens the door.

He says: 'Welcome home, Emile.'

There are stairs on the other side of the door. They walk up the stairs. Nicolas is walking in front and Emile is walking behind him.

They go up one flight of stairs and then they go up another flight of stairs. They are at the top of the stairs. They are standing in front of another door.

Nicolas still has the keys in his hand. He opens the door. They go inside.

They are in an apartment. It is dark.

Nicolas turns on the lights. Emile puts his suitcase down by the door. He puts it down carefully. He takes his knapsack off. He puts it down beside his suitcase.

There is a table in the middle of the apartment. It has four chairs around it. Emile sits down on one of the chairs.

Nicolas takes his jacket off. Emile rubs at his eyes. He is tired. He rubs at his eyes because he does not want to be tired.

Emile starts to make a cigarette.

Nicolas looks at Emile making a cigarette. He says: 'I'm sorry.' He says: 'I need to get to bed.'

Emile says: 'Oh.'

He stops making the cigarette. He says: 'Do not worry about me.' He says: 'I remember my way around.'

Nicolas says: 'Okay. Good night, Emile. I'll see you in the morning.'

Nicolas goes into his bedroom. He closes the door behind him. Emile is still sitting at the table.

He remembers the girl on the platform. She did not wave goodbye.

She was standing on the platform. The train was going to leave. She was wearing a dress with frills around the collar.

She raised a hand to push her hair away from her face.

She did not wave goodbye.

Emile says: 'Good night, Nicolas.'

2

Isobel is standing on the platform of the train station.

The train is gone. The people who got off the train are gone. There is no one here. The woman inside the station is knitting. She is making a sweater. Isobel is alone on the platform.

She is standing at the edge of the platform. She is holding her hands together in front of her. She wants there to be something to look at.

The train is gone. There is nothing to look at.

She is standing at the edge of the platform. It is where she was standing to watch the train go. She stays at the edge of the platform and then she walks away from it.

There is a bench on the platform. She goes to the bench. She sits down on the bench on the platform. She sits with her hands together in her lap. She squeezes her hands together. She does it so hard that her knuckles turn white.

She does not know that her knuckles have turned white. She does not know what to do.

The woman inside the station puts her knitting down. She gets out of the booth she sits in. She has her purse in her hands.

The woman comes out onto the platform.

She sees Isobel. Isobel is sitting on the bench. She does not say anything to Isobel. She walks to the end of the platform.

She reaches into her purse. She takes out a pack of cigarettes. She takes out a cigarette. She puts it to her mouth. She takes a book of matches out of her purse. She lights her cigarette with a match.

She holds the cigarette in her hand and she blows smoke out of her mouth. She looks at Isobel sitting on the bench. Isobel can feel her looking at her.

The woman narrows her eyes.

She finishes smoking her cigarette. She takes a stick of gum out of her purse. She puts it into her mouth.

She goes back inside the station. She walks slowly. She is very fat. Inside the station a radio comes on. There is music playing on the radio. Isobel hears it from where she is sitting on the platform.

Isobel stands up. She stands by the bench for a moment. She does not move. She stands still. It is like she is deciding what she is going to do.

She goes inside the station.

There is a snack machine inside the station. She goes to the snack machine. The woman is here. She is sitting in her booth. She is knitting.

Isobel looks at the woman sitting in the booth as she goes to the snack machine.

Isobel takes some coins out of her pocket. She counts them in her hand. She counts them and then she looks at the snack machine.

The woman behind the pane of glass stops knitting. She looks at Isobel.

Isobel counts the coins in her hand again. She looks at the snack machine again. She makes a decision. She puts some of the coins into it. She presses a button on the front of the machine.

Gears turn inside the machine. It gives her a snack. Isobel looks at the woman behind the pane of glass. The woman is looking at her.

Isobel scowls. She wants to scowl at the woman but she does not. She looks at the ground. She goes back onto the platform.

There is the bench on the platform. She goes to the bench and she sits down on the bench. She eats her snack. While she is eating her snack a train comes. It stops beside the other platform. Isobel stops eating her snack. She looks at the train.

Things happen on the other platform. She cannot see what happens on the other platform. The train is between her and the other platform.

She looks at the train until it leaves.

When the train leaves there is no one left on the other platform. She looks down at her hands. She is holding her snack in her hands.

She starts to eat her snack again.

Someone comes onto the platform. He is pulling a suitcase behind him.

He sees Isobel sitting on the bench. Isobel looks at him. She stops chewing and she looks at him. There is still some of her snack in her mouth.

Isobel is sitting on the only bench on the platform. He does not sit down on the bench. Isobel finishes eating her snack.

She looks at the empty wrapper in her hand. She closes one hand around it. She puts her hands in her lap.

She looks at the man on the platform. He is wearing a cap. He does not sit on the bench. There is room for him to sit on the bench but he does not sit on the bench.

He adjusts his cap. He stands on the platform. Isobel looks at her hands in her lap. The radio in the station is playing music. Her knuckles are white again. She sees that her knuckles are white. She does not want her knuckles to be white.

She stands up. She goes to the end of the platform. She wants to be able to see the trains that have left. She cannot see the trains that have left. They are too far away. She looks back at the bench. Her knuckles are white again. There are tears in her eyes. She looks down.

She is standing where the woman was smoking a cigarette. The butt of her cigarette is still smoking. Isobel scowls.

She does not know why she is still here.

She walks into the station. There are washrooms inside the station. There is a washroom for men and there is a washroom for women. She goes into the washroom for women. There is a sink by the door of the washroom. Behind the sink there are two stalls.

She goes into one of the stalls. She closes the door. She does not lock it. She does not think to lock it. She puts the cover of the toilet down. She sits on the toilet.

She drops her head into her hands. She grabs hold of her hair. She does not know what else to do.

The radio in the station is playing music. The woman in the station hums the tune while it plays. She is sitting behind her pane of glass. She is still knitting.

Isobel is sitting on a toilet with her head in her hands.

She lifts her head. She stands up. She opens the door to the stall. The washroom is empty. She goes to stand in front of the sink. She looks at herself in the mirror.

She scowls. She hates that there is nothing else to do.

She takes some paper towels from beside the sink. She wipes at her eyes. She throws the paper towels into the garbage.

She goes out of the washroom. She goes out of the station. The woman behind the pane of glass watches her. Isobel scowls at her. She knows that she should not. She does not care. She scowls at her and she walks out of the train station.

Outside the train station there is the road that leads to the train station. Isobel stands on the road. She could walk back down the road. It would take her to the town. She does not want to go back to the town.

The train station is behind her. There are the tracks leading away from it. There is the road. There is nowhere else to go.

She walks down the road.

Isobel is standing in front of the grocery store.

She is back in the town. She walked down the main street of the town and now she is standing in front of the grocery store.

There is a sign in the window of the grocery store. It says that the grocery store is closed.

It is late. She does not know where else to go. She tries to open the door.

It is locked.

She is standing in front of the grocery store on the main street of the town. She is not supposed to have a key to the door. She takes the key from her pocket. She opens the door. She goes inside the store.

It is dark inside. She is not supposed to be here. She does not turn on the lights.

She is hungry.

There are vegetables in a basket in front of her. She takes some of the vegetables. She is not sure what the vegetables are. She cannot see them. She walks further into the store. She takes other things out of baskets and off the shelves. She holds them in her arms. She walks to the back of the store. There is a door there. It goes to the room at the back of the store.

The door is not locked. She opens it.

There are no windows in this room. It is too dark to see. Isobel takes a breath. She knows that there are things on the floor of this room. She is not sure where they are. She puts one hand out in front of her. She is holding the food she took in her other arm.

She steps into the room.

Her foot hits something. It hurts. She bites her lip. There are crates scattered around. She knows that there are stairs in this room. They go to the rooms that are above the grocery store.

She takes another step. She is going to where the stairs are.

Her feet hit other things. She stumbles. She drops some of the food she took. She cannot see where it dropped. She does not stop to look for it.

She reaches the bottom of the stairs. She puts her hand on the banister. She goes up the stairs.

One of her hands is on the banister beside the stairs. The other is holding the food she took. At the top of the stairs there is a room. It is not really a room. It is more like an attic. She goes to the top of the stairs. There is a door. She opens the door. She is in the room.

There is a window in one of the walls. There is a curtain over it. The curtain is flimsy. A bit of light from the alley comes through it.

Isobel can see a bed. It is against one wall of the room. She can see a sink on one of the other walls. There is a mirror on the wall over it.

She goes to the middle of the room. There is a light bulb hanging from the ceiling. She cannot see it but she knows it is there. She stands under the light bulb. She reaches up. She pulls on the string hanging from it.

The light bulb turns on.

The bed against the wall is a small bed. There is a bare mattress on the bed frame. It is the bed she woke up in this morning. The plain white sheets are gone. There is not supposed to be anyone here. The sheets have been put away.

Isobel sits down on the floor. The floor is made of planks of wood. She puts the food she took on the floor. She eats some of the food. She uses her hands.

When she is done eating she stands up again. She goes over to the sink. She washes her face. There is not a towel hanging by the sink. There had been a towel there this morning. It has been put away too.

She wants to feel at home here.

She scowls. She has to use her dress to dry her face.

She walks to the middle of the room. She pulls on the string hanging from the light bulb again. The light bulb turns off.

She lies down on the mattress.

She wants to believe she has come home. She is lying on a bare mattress. There are no sheets and no blankets. She is still wearing her dress.

She has not come home.

There is a truck in the alley behind the store. Its engine is running. It is morning. Isobel is lying on the bed. She had been asleep. Now she is awake. The sound of the truck woke her.

She rubs at her eyes. She sits up in the bed. It was cold during the night. She had no blankets. She did not sleep well. Her body is stiff. She is still tired. She stands up. She rubs at her eyes again.

She goes over to the sink. She looks at herself in the mirror. She looks like she just got out of bed. She tries to make her hair look nicer. She pushes at it. It does not make her hair look nicer. She looks like she just got out of bed.

She grits her teeth.

She wants to look nicer.

She turns the water on. She washes her face. She dries her face on her dress again.

She looks at herself in the mirror. She tries to not scowl. She takes a breath. She opens the door and she goes out of the room.

She is above the grocery store. In the room at the back of the grocery store there are two men. They are carrying crates. There are crates in the truck behind the grocery store. The men are carrying the crates from the truck into the store.

Isobel comes down the stairs. She goes into the room at the back of the store. She stands there.

The two men see her.

They look at her.

One of the men says: 'Isobel.' He stops. He says: 'What are you doing here?'

Isobel pulls her hands through her hair. She does not scowl. She lets out a breath.

She says: 'Good morning, Mr. Koch.'

Isobel is sitting on a chair.

She is sitting with her hands between her legs. She is nervous. She is fidgeting because she is nervous. She is trying not to fidget but she cannot keep herself from fidgeting.

Mr. Koch is standing in front of her. He is holding two cups of coffee.

He gives Isobel one of the cups of coffee.

Mr. Koch is the owner of the grocery store. This is his office. It is a small room at the back of the grocery store.

There is a desk in the office. There is a desk and a machine for making coffee and a chair behind the desk and the chair Isobel is sitting in.

Mr. Koch sits down behind his desk. He grunts when he sits down. Isobel is sitting in front of his desk. Mr. Koch looks at her. She is holding her cup of coffee with both hands.

Mr. Koch makes a noise in his throat.

He takes a cigarette from the pack of cigarettes on his desk. His hair is grey. He is not young. He was thin when he was young. Now he is not. He is fat.

He puts the cigarette to his mouth. He lights it. Smoke comes out of his mouth.

Isobel does not look at Mr. Koch. She holds her cup of coffee in her lap. She uses both hands. She should look at Mr. Koch but she looks into her cup of coffee instead.

She lifts her cup of coffee to her mouth. She takes a sip from it.

Mr. Koch puts his cigarette to his mouth. He coughs. He looks at Isobel. He says: 'What are you doing here?'

Isobel says: 'I could work for you.' She does not look up. Her hair falls into her face. She does not move her hair out of her face. She feels safer with her hair in her face.

Mr. Koch does not hear what she said. He says: 'Excuse me?'

Isobel looks into her cup of coffee. There are ripples on the surface of the coffee. Her cup is shaking. Her cup is shaking because her hands are shaking. She tries to hold her hands still.

Isobel says: 'I could work for you.'

Mr. Koch shakes his head. He makes a noise in his throat. He puts his hand to his mouth. He coughs.

Isobel does not say anything.

Mr. Koch puts his cigarette to his mouth. He draws on it. He takes his cigarette away from his mouth. Smoke comes out of his mouth.

It is a small room. It does not have a window.

Mr. Koch says: 'Don't be ridiculous.' He shakes his head again. He says: 'You're too young.'

Isobel does not look at him.

He says: 'Isobel, go back to your family.'

Isobel says: 'No.'

She says: 'I don't want to.' She says: 'I could work for you.'

Mr. Koch grumbles. He says: 'You are too young for that.'

She says: 'No.'

Mr. Koch says: 'What will happen when your mother finds you here?'

Isobel's shoulders sink. She looks into her cup of coffee.

Mr. Koch says: 'What would I say to her?'

Isobel does not look up. She looks into her cup of coffee and she says: 'No.' She says it softly. She is trying to keep her hands still. She does not want her cup of coffee to shake.

Her cup of coffee is shaking.

Mr. Koch is looking at her. She knows that Mr. Koch is looking at her. She does not look at him. She wants more of her hair to fall into her face.

She should move her hair so it is not in her face. She should look at Mr. Koch.

She raises a hand to her hair. It is thick and almost black.

She wants more of her hair to fall into her face. She grabs a handful of it.

Mr. Koch looks at her hand move. He puts his cigarette to his mouth. He draws on it. He takes his cigarette away from his mouth.

Isobel does not say anything.

Mr. Koch says: 'What would I say to her?' Smoke comes out of his mouth.

He coughs. It is a wet cough.

Isobel does not say anything. One of her hands is in her hair. She pulls it.

Mr. Koch makes more noises in his throat. He puts his cigarette to his mouth. He draws deeply on it. It makes him cough.

He shakes his head.

He stops coughing. He says: 'It is impossible.'

Isobel pulls her hair over her face. She has to look at Mr. Koch. She knows she has to look at Mr. Koch. She cannot pull her hair over her face. She is pulling her hair over her face.

She moves her hand so it is pushing at her hair. She pushes her hair onto the top of her head.

She is still looking into her cup of coffee. She is holding it with one hand. Her other hand is holding on to her hair.

She has to look up. She is pale. Her eyes are open too wide. She is grinding her teeth together.

Mr. Koch sees her hands moving her hair. He drinks from his cup of coffee. He makes a noise in his throat.

Mr. Koch says: 'What would you do?'

Isobel stops pushing at her hair. She does not understand. If she looked at him she would understand. She does not look at him. She cannot look at him. She is afraid.

She says: 'What?' It is a whisper.

Mr. Koch says: 'If you worked for me. What would you do?'

She lets go of her hair. It falls into her face. She still does not look at Mr. Koch. Mr. Koch is looking at her. Under her dress, she is sweating. He puts his cigarette to his mouth. Isobel looks into her cup of coffee.

She does not say anything. Her shoulders drop.

Mr. Koch takes his cigarette from his mouth. He says: 'What would you do?'

Isobel says: 'I don't know.'

Mr. Koch blows smoke into the room. He coughs.

He says: 'You see?'

He puts his cigarette to his mouth. He is still coughing. He draws on his cigarette.

He says: 'It is not possible.'

Mr. Koch says: 'It is not possible.' He says: 'And that is that.'

He puts out his cigarette. There is an ashtray on his desk. It is filled with cigarette butts. He starts to stand.

Isobel says: 'No.'

She looks at Mr. Koch. It hurts her. She looks at him.

She says: 'No.'

She says: 'I could work for you.'

Mr Koch says: 'Isobel.' He says: 'Be reasonable.'

He says: 'Go back to your family. What you've done doesn't matter. They will take you back. They are your family.'

Isobel says: 'No.'

Mr. Koch looks at Isobel. He says: 'You cannot ask me to do this.'

Isobel's coffee spills. She can feel it through her dress. It is hot. She does not breathe.

Isobel says: 'I could work for you.'

Mr. Koch looks at Isobel. Her mouth is trembling. She is going to cry. She is not going to cry. She will not. Her eyes are hard.

Mr. Koch is not well. He is old. He makes noises in his throat. He coughs.

He drinks from his cup of coffee. Isobel looks at him. Mr. Koch grumbles.

He says: 'It is not a simple thing you are asking.'

Isobel says: 'I could work for you.'

Mr. Koch sighs. He shakes his head. He coughs into his hand.

Mr. Koch says: 'There are crates in the back.'

He stands up. He is old. He stands up slowly. It is getting harder for him to stand up. He is old and he weighs too much. He starts to move towards the door.

He says: 'You could help me unpack them.'

Dear Emile,

I am in the train station.

I am sitting on the bench. I don't know what else to do. There isn't anything for me to do. I would still be standing where I was when I watched you go, but my legs are tired.

It is 11:37.

I feel like I'm waiting for something. Something that I could remember this by. I don't know what it could be. It's 11:37. That is what it says on the clock here. For a while, I wanted 11:37 to be enough. But it's not. I want something more.

It's 11:38. It will be 11:39 soon. I am still sitting here. I want something that will make this mean something. I want something that makes all of this worth it.

The woman who works in the station, she was at the end of the platform smoking a cigarette. It was a little while ago. She was looking at me like there was something wrong with me. When she was done she dropped the cigarette on the platform. She looked at me one more time and then she went back to whatever it is that she does here.

I went to where she'd been. I picked up the butt of her cigarette. It will have to do.

I love you.

3

Emile is walking down a street.

It is a busy street. There are people walking down the street and there are other people standing in the street. They are wearing scarves. They are huddled inside their jackets. The street is crowded with people huddled inside their jackets.

He walks past a news stand. There is a woman standing behind the news stand. She is talking with a man standing in front of the news stand.

Emile is wearing a jacket and a grey cap. He has his hands stuffed in his pockets. It is getting cold. He is looking at the sidewalk in front of him. He does not look at the man and the woman at the news stand. He walks past them.

He does not look at anybody on the street. His cap is pulled down. He looks at the sidewalk. He does not listen to what people are saying.

There is an old woman walking a dog. She is holding the dog's leash in her hand. Her hand is trembling. She cannot help it. She is old.

Emile is going to a café. He is meeting someone named Agatha. There is a reel of film tucked under his arm. He will give it to Agatha. They will talk to each other. They have not seen each other in a long time. They have things to say. Then she will take the reel of film away to be developed.

The dog is an old dog. It cannot walk quickly. It is trying to walk quickly. It is wheezing. So is the old woman.

Emile walks past the old woman walking her dog. There are too many people in the street. He bumps her elbow. He does not stop to say that he is sorry. He does not slow down.

He has to be on the other side of the street. He crosses the street. He is almost at the café. He walks past a bookstore. There are cats in the windows of the bookstore. He walks past a laundromat. There are people sitting in the laundromat. They are not doing anything. They are waiting for their laundry to finish.

One of the people in the laundromat watches Emile walk past the window.

The café is on the other side of the laundromat. Emile walks past the laundromat. He goes into the café.

Emile takes his cap off. He holds it in his hands. He is still wearing his jacket. He does not want to take his jacket off. He does not want to be exposed. He is standing in the door to the café. He looks inside. He does not step inside. He looks inside.

He does not see Agatha. He wonders if he is early. He does not have a watch so he cannot tell. He does not want to be early. He does not know if he is early. He does not want to be late.

He steps inside the café.

There is smoke hanging in the air. There are too many people in the café. There is not much light. Emile cannot see an empty table.

There is an empty table in the back of the café. Emile's eyes get used to the light. He sees the empty table. He walks over to it. It is beside two old men. The old men are sitting at a table playing backgammon.

Emile says: 'Is someone sitting here?'

One of the old men looks up from the game. His tie is loose. The top button of his shirt is open.

The old man waves his hand towards the table.

He goes back to his game.

The other old man rolls the dice. Emile sits down at the table. He puts the reel of film on the table. He takes off his jacket. He puts it over the back of his chair. He looks around the café. Agatha is supposed to be here.

He does not see Agatha. The other old man rolls the dice.

Emile stands up. He goes to the counter. He stands at the counter. A barista sees him standing at the counter. She goes over to Emile.

Emile says: 'I would like a coffee.' He gives her some money. He goes back to his table.

One of the old men rolls the dice. The barista brings Emile a coffee. Emile is watching the old men play. He does not see his coffee arrive. He looks away from the game and there is a cup in front of him.

The cup is on a saucer. There is a spoon on the saucer. It is beside the cup. There is a bowl of sugar on the table. Emile puts the spoon into the bowl of sugar. He puts some of the sugar into the coffee. He stirs the coffee with the spoon.

He lifts the cup to his mouth. He sips from the cup. He puts the cup back on the saucer.

The old men roll the dice. Emile does not look at them. He picks up his cup of coffee. He does not look around the café.

He puts his elbows on the table. He holds his cup of coffee in his hands. He looks at the coffee inside the cup.

He waits for Agatha.

Agatha says: 'I'm so sorry I'm late.'

Emile looks up from his cup. He is surprised. He did not see Agatha come into the café.

Agatha says: 'Hello, Emile.'

Emile puts his cup of coffee onto its saucer. He puts his hands on the table.

He says: 'Hello, Agatha.'

Agatha smiles. She says: 'Emile, give me a kiss.'

Emile moves his chair away from the table. He stands up.

He steps towards Agatha. She puts her hand on his arm. She leans towards him. He kisses her on one cheek and then he kisses her on the other cheek.

Agatha keeps her hands on Emile's arms. She says: 'You've been gone so long.' She squeezes him. She says: 'I'm so glad to see you again.'

Emile nods his head. He smiles. He is not sure he wants to smile the way that he is smiling. He smiles anyway.

He sits down. He pulls his chair closer to the table.

The old men playing backgammon stop playing. They look at Agatha. She has red hair. She wears it piled on top of her head. It is very dramatic.

Emile moves his cup of coffee closer to him. Agatha sees it. She says: 'Come, Emile. You've been gone so long.' She smiles. She says: 'The occasion calls for something more than coffee.'

She has her purse in her hands. She goes to the counter. She talks to the people standing behind the counter.

Emile hears her laugh.

She comes back to the table. She sits down across from Emile. She sits so her legs are not under the table. She takes a cigarette from her purse. She puts it to her mouth.

She rests an elbow on the table. She crosses her legs.

The old men are still looking at Agatha. They are looking at her legs. She has very long legs. She does not look at the old men. One of them shakes his head. He clears his throat. He picks up the dice and he rolls them.

Agatha lights her cigarette. She leans back in her chair. She puts one of her arms over the back of it. She smiles at Emile.

The barista brings a carafe of wine over. She puts it between Agatha and Emile. She puts a glass down in front of Emile and a glass down in front of Agatha.

Agatha picks up the carafe. She pours some wine into the glass in front of Emile. She pours some wine into her glass.

She picks up her glass.

She says: 'Welcome home, Emile.' Emile picks up his glass. They touch their glasses together. She says: 'We've missed you.'

Emile looks down. He smiles. He does not say anything. He drinks from his glass. It is cheap wine. It does not taste very good. It is that kind of café. They cannot afford to go anywhere else. They have learned to like it.

Agatha drinks from her glass. She puts it back on the table. She looks at the reel of film on the table and then she looks at Emile.

She says: 'Did you get it done?'

Emile nods his head.

He picks up the reel of film. He gives it to Agatha. She holds it in her hands.

Agatha says: 'Did it work out?'

Emile says: 'I think so.'

Agatha says: 'Good.' She says: 'You're just in time for the festival.'

She puts the film next to her purse. She picks up her glass. She drinks from it.

She says: 'You will come, won't you?'

Emile is a puppeteer. He makes shows with puppets.

Agatha went to see one of Emile's shows. It was before Emile left. She sat down in a theatre. She crossed her legs. The curtains opened. She watched the show.

When the show was done she walked up to Emile. She said: 'I liked your show.' She said: 'You should make a film.'

Emile said: 'I don't have a camera.'

Agatha said: 'Don't worry. I can get you a camera.'

She met Emile in a bar. They drank a bottle of wine together. They left the bar.

They stood in the street outside the bar. It was late. Agatha took a pack of cigarettes out of her purse. She put one of the cigarettes to her lips. She was carrying a small case. It was closed with clasps. It had a handle on it for carrying. She gave Emile the case.

She said: 'The camera's inside.'

Agatha lit the cigarette. She used a lighter. They were both drunk from the wine.

Emile said: 'How does it work?'

Agatha said: 'You don't know?'

Emile said: 'No.'

It was a warm night. It was almost summer. Emile and Agatha were not wearing jackets. Agatha's shoulders were bare.

Agatha said: 'Well.' She put her cigarette to her lips. She drew on it. She dropped it onto the sidewalk. She took a tube of lipstick out of her purse. She put lipstick on her lips. It was very red lipstick.

She said: 'Come to my place. I'll show you how it works.'

She put her arm in Emile's arm. They walked together down the street.

Emile passed out on Agatha's couch.

It was after they went to the bar. The camera was on the table in front of the couch. Agatha had shown Emile how it worked. There was a bottle of brandy on the table beside it.

Agatha was standing beside Emile. She was holding a blanket. She bent over him. She touched his hair, gently. She put the blanket over him.

Agatha was drunk. Some of her hair was still piled on top of her head. The rest of her hair was falling onto her shoulders.

She walked away from the couch. She did not walk steadily. She kept one hand touching the wall. She went into her bedroom.

In the morning they sat in Agatha's kitchen. Emile wore the clothes he wore the night before. He was wearing a white shirt and a worn pair of trousers. He had slept in them. They were rumpled. He was rumpled. Agatha was wearing a dressing gown.

They sat in Agatha's kitchen. They drank coffee. Agatha lit a cigarette. She gave it to Emile. He smoked some of it. He gave it back to Agatha.

They did not say anything.

The window in Agatha's kitchen looked over an alley. There was a dog barking outside.

Agatha and Emile sat in the kitchen. They drank coffee. Agatha said: 'Do you want anything?' She looked at Emile. He did not say anything. She said: 'Breakfast?'

Emile shook his head. Agatha's dressing gown was made of something like silk. It had Japanese flowers printed on it.

They drank coffee. They did not say anything. Agatha's legs were bare. Emile did not know if Agatha was wearing anything under her dressing gown. Agatha stood up.

She said: 'I'm going to have a shower. I'll be quick.'

She went into the bathroom. She closed the door. Emile sat at the table. He heard her turn the shower on. He stood up from the table.

He put the camera into its case. He went to the bathroom door. He said: 'I am going.'

Agatha said: 'What?'

Emile said: 'I am going.'

Agatha said: 'Emile, I can't hear you.'

She said: 'Come in.'

Emile had the case in his hands. He walked to the door that went down to the street. He put on his shoes.

He left.

Emile and Agatha are sitting in a café. There is a carafe of wine on the table between them. There is no wine left in the carafe.

There are two glasses on the table. They are empty.

Agatha leans back in her chair. She says: 'Oh, Emile. I don't want to say it, but I should be going. I have so much to do for the festival.'

Emile nods his head. They stand up.

Agatha is taller than Emile. She is wearing high-heeled shoes. They make her even taller. They walk out of the café.

They stand in the street.

Emile says: 'I liked making the film.' He does not look at Agatha. He looks at the sidewalk.

Agatha says: 'Then keep the camera.' It is cold out. Emile and Agatha are wearing their jackets. Agatha's jacket has fur around the collar.

Agatha smiles. She says: 'Make another one. Do us all proud.'

Agatha has a wolfish smile. It makes her teeth look sharp.

It is getting late.

It is not late yet. It is only getting late.

Emile turns up his collar. He is standing on the street outside the café. Inside, the old men are still playing backgammon. Agatha has left. When she left she put her hand on his arm and she leaned over towards him. He kissed her on one cheek and then he kissed her on the other cheek.

She said: 'Goodbye, Emile.' She winked at him. She said: 'I'll see you soon.'

She left. She walked away down the street.

Emile is still standing on the street in front of the café.

He does not know where to go. There are not as many people on the street. They have gone home. A couple walks past him. They are young. They are holding hands. One of them says something. The other one laughs.

Emile could go home.

He walks down the street. There is a stop for the streetcar at the end of the street. The couple that walked past Emile is standing at the stop. They are standing close to each other. There is a woman watching them. She has a purse. She is holding her purse with both of her hands.

Emile stops. He waits for the streetcar.

A streetcar comes. It stops. The people standing at the stop get on. Emile gets on with them. He puts some money into the fare machine. The driver gives him a ticket. He finds a seat. He sits down.

The streetcar moves and then the streetcar stops. The doors open. People get on the streetcar. The doors close. The streetcar moves again. The streetcar stops. Emile stands up. The doors open. He goes to the doors. He gets off the streetcar. He is standing on a platform in the middle of the street.

He crosses the street. It is starting to get dark. He walks down the street and then he stops. There are shops on either side of him. They are closed for the night. He is standing in front of a door between them.

He opens the door. He goes inside. There are stairs inside. He goes up the stairs. There are two flights of stairs inside. He goes all the way up the stairs. He comes to a door. He opens the door. He goes inside.

He is home.

Nicolas is not at home. He is working at the bar. Emile turns the lights on. He takes his jacket and his cap off. He hangs them on a hook in the wall.

There is a table in the middle of the apartment. There are four chairs around it.

Emile sits at the table.

There are apples and oranges on the table. They are in a bowl.

Emile takes some of the apples and some of the oranges out of the bowl. He puts them one in front of the other.

He puts them so that they are in a row pointing away from him.

He picks up the apple at one end of the row and he moves it forward slightly. He stands up to do it. He picks up the apple behind it and moves it forward slightly. He picks up the orange behind it and moves it forward slightly.

He moves all of the apples and oranges again. He sits down again. The apples and oranges are further away from him.

He wants to know what it is like to watch someone leave. He stands up again. He moves the apples and oranges again.

They are further away from where he was sitting.

He sits down again. He stands up again. He moves the apples and the oranges further away. He moves faster.

He keeps moving them until they fall off the end of the table.

He wants the sound of the fruit hitting the floor to be like the sound of a train. It is not the sound of a train. It is the sound of fruit hitting the floor.

He sits at the table. He puts his hands on top of the table. He looks where the fruit was.

It is what it is like to watch someone leave.

Nicolas comes home.

Emile is sitting at the table. His hands are on the table in front of him. There are apples and oranges on the floor.

Nicolas picks one of the apples up off the floor. He looks at it.

Nicolas shakes his head. He says: 'Emile, they're bruised.'

Emile looks at Nicolas. His hands are still on the table. Nicolas puts the apple he picked up into the bowl on the table.

Emile says: 'Oh.'

Nicolas goes into his bedroom.

Emile stands up. He walks to where the apples and oranges fell. He bends down. He picks up an apple. He looks to see if it is bruised.

It is bruised.

He picks up the apples and the oranges. He puts them back in the bowl on the table. He goes over to Nicolas's bedroom. The door is closed.

He says: 'I'm sorry.'

Nicolas does not answer. Emile wonders if Nicolas heard him. He wonders if he should say he is sorry again. He does not say he is sorry again.

He turns out the lights. He goes into his bedroom.

~ 4 ~

There is a bed here.

The bed has plain white sheets on it again. Isobel is lying under the sheets. They are tangled around her body. She is asleep.

It is morning. Last night Isobel got into the bed. She fell asleep. It was late when she fell asleep. She did not want to sleep. She knew she would have nightmares if she fell asleep. She did not want to have nightmares.

She tried to stop herself from dreaming. She turned her head away. She twisted and kicked with her legs. It did not work. Now it is morning. There is a window above the bed. There is light coming in through the window. There are specks of dust floating in the light.

There is a truck under the window. It is in the alley behind the store. Isobel hears the truck.

She is lying twisted in the bed. The sheets are tangled around her body.

She opens her eyes.

She has to be awake now. She closes her eyes again. She does not want to be awake. She is tired. Fighting her nightmares makes her tired. She rubs at her face with her hands. It does not change anything.

She is tired and she has to be awake now.

She sits up in the bed. She runs her hands through her hair. Her hair is tangled. It is matted against her head. She pulls her hands through her hair until it is less tangled.

She is in the room over the grocery store. There is a bed in the room. There is a sink. There is a window. There is a door.

She stands up. She is awake. She does not feel awake. She is standing beside the bed. She goes over to the sink. She looks into the mirror. There is a mirror over the sink.

She sees herself looking in the mirror. There are dark creases under her eyes.

She scowls.

She does not want there to be dark creases under her eyes. She wants her sleep to be better than this. She does not know how to make it better. She looks down. She fills the sink with water. She washes her face in the sink. She reaches for the towel hanging beside the sink. She dries her face.

She walks away from the sink. Her dress is on the floor. She picks it up. She smells it. It does not smell good. She puts it on the bed.

She looks at her dress lying on the bed. It is limp and shapeless and dirty. It should be washed. She pulls her hands through her hair. It is less tangled than it was when she woke up. It is still tangled. She pulls her hands through her hair until it is less tangled.

She puts her dress on. Her shoes are by the door. She goes over to the door. She puts her shoes on. She goes through the door.

She is standing at the top of the stairs. There is a window in the ceiling over them. Light is coming in through the window. There is dust floating in the light. The dust reminds her of other things.

She wishes that she were not so tired.

Isobel's dress has frills on it. They go around the collar. She goes down the stairs.

At the bottom of the stairs is the room at the back of the grocery store. The room is full of crates. There are crates with nothing in them and there are crates with things in them.

There is a door going out to the alley. It is propped open. Mr. Koch comes in through the door. He is carrying a crate. It is a crate with things in it. He puts the crate down. His face is red. He sees Isobel.

Another man comes in through the back door. He is a young man. He is not that much older than Isobel. He is carrying a crate. He puts it down next to the crate Mr. Koch brought in.

They are making a pile of crates next to the door.

Mr. Koch says: 'Isobel, this is Oskar.' He turns and he says: 'Oskar, this is Isobel.'

Oskar says: 'Hello, Isobel.' He holds out his hand.

Isobel looks at Oskar's hand. She puts out her hand the way he put out his hand. She does not step towards him. She does not know that she should. She is too young. He steps towards her. He takes her hand. He shakes it.

Isobel says: 'Hello.'

Oskar lets go of Isobel's hand. Oskar and Mr. Koch go back out the door. Isobel follows them out the door. There is a truck in the alley behind the grocery store. It is backed up next to the door.

Oskar gets into the back of the truck.

There are crates in the back of the truck. He hands a crate to Mr. Koch. Mr. Koch takes the crate. He grunts when he does. He goes into the grocery store carrying the crate.

Oskar picks up a crate to hand to Isobel. He says: 'Be careful, it's heavy.'

Isobel is too thin. She does not look like she is very strong. She cannot help that she is thin. She scowls.

Isobel says: 'I'll be okay.'

She takes the crate. It is too heavy for her. She takes it inside the store.

Mr. Koch is inside the store. He puts the crate he is carrying down. Isobel puts the crate she is carrying next to the crate Mr. Koch put down.

Oskar comes into the store after Isobel. He is carrying a crate. He puts the crate he is carrying on top of the crate Mr. Koch put down.

They stand inside the store. Mr. Koch is breathing hard. They look at each other.

Mr. Koch says: 'Well, come on.' He smiles. His face is red. He hitches the waist of his pants up. He goes back out into the alley. Isobel and Oskar follow him.

Oskar gets into the back of the truck. There are crates in the back of the truck. Oskar hands a crate to Mr. Koch.

Mr. Koch takes the crate and goes back into the store. He is still breathing heavily.

Oskar hands a crate to Isobel. She takes the crate inside the store.

There are steps going from the alley up to the door. Isobel slips on the steps. She slips but she does not fall.

Oskar sees her slip. He says: 'Isobel!' He sees that she did not fall. He says: 'Be careful.'

Isobel says: 'I'm fine.'

She stops on the steps. She changes how she is holding the crate. She does not want to drop it. She is not sure how to carry it.

She starts walking up the steps again. She goes into the store. She puts the crate she is carrying next to the crate Mr. Koch put down. She puts it down and she leans on it.

Mr. Koch is still inside. He pats Isobel on the shoulder.

Isobel does not look at him. She leans on the crate. She puts her hand into her hair. Oskar comes into the store. He is carrying a crate. He puts the crate he is carrying on top of the crate Mr. Koch was carrying.

Oskar looks at Isobel. She is scowling. He does not say anything. Mr. Koch and Oskar go back outside. Isobel pushes her hair out of her face. She has to go out to the truck. She has to do it. She follows Oskar and Mr. Koch. Oskar gets into the back of the truck.

Oskar hands a crate to Mr. Koch. He hands a crate to Isobel. They go back inside the store. Oskar picks a crate up. He follows them into the store.

They do this until there are no more crates in the back of Oskar's truck.

When there are no more crates in the back of Oskar's truck Oskar closes the doors that go into the back of the truck. He takes off the gloves that he wears while he carries crates. He puts them into the pockets of his overalls. He adjusts his cap.

He says: 'Goodbye, Mr. Koch.' He says: 'Goodbye, Isobel.'

Mr. Koch says: 'Say hello to your father for me. Tell him I miss seeing him.'

Oskar gets into the front of the truck. He closes the door. He starts the truck's engine. Mr. Koch waves his hand. Oskar reaches his hand out of the window and he waves to Mr. Koch.

The truck drives away down the alley.

Isobel and Mr. Koch go back into the grocery store. Mr. Koch closes the door. They are in the room at the back of the store. There are crates piled beside them. Mr. Koch wipes his face. He puts his handkerchief in his pocket.

He says: 'Shall we have a cup of coffee?'

Isobel is sitting on a crate. Her arms hurt. Her back hurts. She is looking at the floor in front of her. She did not know it would hurt like this.

Isobel does not say anything.

Mr. Koch makes a noise in his throat. He says: 'Shall we have a cup of coffee before we get to work?'

Isobel looks up. Mr. Koch is waiting for her to answer. She has to say something.

She says: 'Yes, please.' She does not say it right away. She thinks about it. She does not push her hair out of her face. She does not like coffee.

She says: 'Yes, please.'

Mr. Koch goes into his office. It is under the stairs that go to the room above the store. He goes into his office and starts his coffee-making machine.

Isobel is still sitting on a crate. She looks at the floor in front of her. She touches herself where she hurts. She touches herself gingerly.

She is not used to hurting like this. She is trying to make sense of it.

Mr. Koch comes out of his office. He is humming a tune to himself. He is carrying two cups of coffee. He is carrying one in each hand. He offers one of them to Isobel.

Isobel is looking at the ground in front of her. Her hair is in her face. She does not see the cup Mr. Koch is holding out to her.

Mr. Koch says: 'Isobel.'

Isobel looks up. She looks at Mr. Koch through her hair. She sees him smiling. She sees the cup of coffee he is holding out to her. She pushes her hair out of her face. She holds her hands out.

Mr. Koch gives her the cup of coffee.

The cup is hot in her hands. It is uncomfortable. Isobel looks into the cup. The coffee inside it is black. Mr. Koch makes a sound in his throat. He says: 'I forgot to ask if you take cream or sugar.'

Isobel says: 'It's okay.'

Mr. Koch goes over to a crate. He hitches his pants up. He sits down on the crate. He brings his cup of coffee up to his mouth. He drinks from it.

He makes a sound in the back of his throat.

He puts his cup of coffee down on the crate beside him. He reaches into the pocket of his waistcoat. He wears a waistcoat when he works. He wears a waistcoat and a shirt and a tie. He takes a pack of cigarettes out from the pocket of his waistcoat.

He puts a cigarette in his mouth. He takes a lighter out of his pocket. He lights the cigarette. He takes the cigarette away from his mouth and he blows smoke into the room.

He settles into sitting on the crate. He scratches his belly.

Mr. Koch says: 'It is good to start the day with someone.'

He picks up his cup of coffee. He drinks from it. He puts it down on the crate next to him.

He sighs.

Mr. Koch says: 'When Emile left, I thought I would be by myself again. And I wasn't looking forward to making do without someone to lend a hand.'

Isobel does not say anything. She watches Mr. Koch speak. Mr. Koch says: 'I suppose I am glad you are here.'

He puts his cigarette in his mouth. He draws on it. He takes his cigarette out of his mouth. He blows smoke into the room.

He does not say Isobel being here will cause trouble. He shakes his head.

Isobel waits for him to say more. She waits but he does not say more.

Mr. Koch sits on one of the crates. He drinks from his cup of coffee. He smokes his cigarette. He makes noises in the back of his throat.

Isobel sips from her cup of coffee. She wants Mr. Koch to say more. She wants to ask Mr. Koch to say something. She does not know how to ask Mr. Koch to say something.

She sips from her cup of coffee.

She does not like the taste of it. It is bitter. She wants to learn to like it. She decides she will learn to like it.

She holds her cup of coffee in her lap. She does not say anything. She sips from her cup of coffee. She watches Mr. Koch sitting on a crate. He drinks from his cup of coffee and he smokes his cigarette.

He puts his cigarette to his mouth one last time. He stands up. He grunts when he stands up.

Mr. Koch says: 'Well.'

Mr. Koch says: 'It's time to get to work.'

There are crates in the room at the back of the grocery store.

Isobel is sitting on one of the crates. She is holding a cup of coffee in her hands. She sips from the cup. She looks around the room. Mr. Koch is in his office. He is working. She is alone here.

She sips from the cup again. She makes a face. She puts it down. There is still coffee in the cup. She cannot drink the rest. It is too bitter.

She stands up.

She goes over to the crates piled near the back door. They are the crates she helped to bring in. She opens the crate on the top of the pile. It is filled with tins. She takes the tins out of the crate.

She takes them over to the door that goes into the store. There is a cart there.

She puts the tins from the crate onto the cart. She goes back to where the crate is. She takes more tins out of the crate. She takes them over to the cart and she puts them on it.

Isobel pushes the cart through the door. She goes into the store. There are rows of shelves here. There are aisles between the shelves. She pushes the cart ahead of her. She goes into the aisles.

There are tins on the shelves along the aisle. She takes some of the tins from the cart. She puts them onto the shelves.

She pushes the cart again. She stops again. She puts some of the tins on the shelves. She pushes the cart again.

There are people in the store. They are shopping for groceries. There is a girl at the front of the store. She is standing behind the cash register. Isobel does not want any of them to notice her. The people shopping for groceries do not notice her. The people do not care about Isobel. They are shopping for groceries.

The girl looks at Isobel. She heard what Isobel did. She does not say anything. She stares at her. Isobel does not say anything. She puts more tins from the cart onto the shelves. She wants to scowl. She does not scowl. She puts tins on the shelves until there are no more tins on the cart.

When there are no more tins on the cart she goes to the back of the store. She leaves the cart by the door. She goes to where the crates are. She takes tins out of the open crate. She takes them over to the cart. She puts them onto the cart.

All the tins left in this crate fit onto the cart. There is still room on the cart. She opens another crate. There are boxes of biscuits and more tins in the crate. She takes the tins out of the crate and she puts them on the cart. With these tins on it the cart is full.

She takes the cart into the front of the store. There are fewer people in the store. One of them has her son with her. He is a little boy. He is holding on to her skirt. Isobel puts the tins from the cart on the shelves. When the cart is empty she goes into the back of the store.

There are more crates in the back of the store. They all have things in them.

Isobel takes the boxes of biscuits from the open crate. They do not fill the cart. She opens the next crate. She takes the things inside it and she puts them on the cart. She takes the cart into the front of the store. She puts the things from the cart onto the shelves.

When all of the things from the cart are on the shelves she goes into the back of the store. She opens another crate.

She does this until all the crates are empty.

Isobel is in the room at the back of the grocery store. There are stairs here. There is a bathroom under the stairs. It is beside Mr. Koch's office. She goes into the bathroom. The stairs are over her head. She washes her hands. They are dirty from working. She dries them on the towel that is here.

She comes out of the bathroom and she goes up the stairs.

Upstairs there is a room. There is a bed and a sink and a window inside it. There are plain white sheets on the bed. There is a mirror on the wall above the sink. There are curtains over the window. The curtains are flimsy.

Isobel closes the door at the top of the stairs behind her. She takes her shoes off. She leaves them beside the door.

She leans against the door. It is a large room. It is cold and there is dust in the corners.

It is late. It is dark outside. There is street light coming in through the curtains. There is not much street light coming in through the curtains. It is dark in the room. Isobel cannot see what is inside the room. She can see the shapes of the things in the room but she cannot see them.

She goes to where the bed is. She does not have to see the bed. She knows where it is. She sits down on the bed.

It is her room now.

She should be glad that it is her room now. She is not sure that she is glad.

She rests her head in her hands. Her body hurts. She has not worked like this before. She went to school. She sat in a desk. She does not want her body to hurt. She does not know what she can do to make her body stop hurting.

She rests her head in her hands. Mr. Koch stands at the bottom of the stairs. He is wearing his jacket and a hat. The hat is a very smart-looking hat.

He says: 'Isobel.' He says: 'Isobel, we're closing up for the day.'

Isobel hears him. She does not say anything. She rests her head in her hands. Her fingers work into her hair. She wants to be able to do this.

Mr. Koch says: 'Will you be all right for the night?' Isobel does not say anything. Mr. Koch says: 'Do you need anything?'

Isobel sits on the bed. She works her fingers deeper into her hair. She makes her hands into fists and she pulls.

Mr. Koch says: 'I will see you in the morning.' He says: 'Good night, Isobel.'

She does not say: 'Good night, Mr. Koch.'

She hears Mr. Koch go out the door that leads into the alley. She hears him close the door behind him. She hears him lock it.

She could look out the window and see him walking away.

She pushes her hair away from her face. She stands up. There is a light bulb hanging from the ceiling. She goes to the middle of the room. She is standing under the light bulb. There is a cord dangling from it. She pulls the cord.

The light turns on.

Isobel is standing in the middle of the room. She does not stand up straight. She is stooped over. She does not want to stand up straight. Her body hurts. She turns towards the sink.

There is a mirror over the sink. She does not want to look into it. She is wearing a nice dress. There are frills around the collar. It is what she wore to the train station.

She wanted to look nice.

The dress is dirty now. She does not have anything else to wear. She does not want to see herself.

She goes to the sink. She pushes her hair away from her face. She washes her face in the sink. She dries her face with the towel hanging next to the sink. There is a towel hanging next to the sink.

She goes back to the bed.

She undoes the buttons on her dress. She lets it drop to the floor. She crawls into the bed.

She wants something else to wear.

She pulls the blanket over herself. She tries to go to sleep.

Emile, I am here.

I am back in your room over the shop. I am here. I wasn't sure that I would come, I wasn't sure that I wouldn't end up back at my mother's house. I know that I said that I wouldn't, but even when I said it I didn't know if I had the courage to really do it.

I did it.

I walked from the train station. I came to the store and I went inside. I went up the stairs.

It was dark. I was afraid to turn the light on. I was afraid that I would be found. I didn't know what would happen if someone found me. And I wanted to have that one night. I needed it.

I was sitting on your bed. Your bed. I spent the night drinking it all in, so that I will remember everything.

The whole night, my heart was racing. I was terrified and exhilarated and I felt alive, Emile. Cold and hungry and alone and alive.

I felt alive.

I am living here now. I'm going to be working for Mr. Koch. But it doesn't matter what happens now. I did it. And I will remember it. Whatever happens will be worth it, so long as I can remember that.

I love you.

Emile is sitting in a theatre.

Nicolas is not sitting beside him. There are people he does not know sitting beside him. On one side there is someone wearing a hat. On the other is someone with dark brown hair.

He does not know who these people are. He does not think that he had ever seen them before they sat down beside him. Emile is sitting between them. His hands are folded in his lap. He is trying to be calm.

He is waiting for the lights to go out.

The lights go out.

The people in the theatre were talking. They stop talking. It is quiet. Emile makes his hands relax. He rests the palms of his hands on top of his legs.

Everyone looks at the front of the theatre. Emile's palms are wet. He wipes them on his trousers. It is a movie theatre. A spotlight turns on in front of the screen.

Someone stands up. She walks to the front of the theatre. She is wearing a nice dress and high-heeled shoes. She does not walk steadily. It is like she is not sure how to walk in high-heeled shoes.

It is Agatha. She is nervous.

Agatha walks to where the light is on in front of the screen. There is a microphone on a stand there. She is carrying a piece of paper in her hand.

She speaks into the microphone. She says what is going to happen. There are going to be short films. They are going to play one after the other.

She says the names of the films. She reads them off the piece of paper in her hand. After she says the name of each film she says the names of the people who made it. Her hair is piled on top of her head. There is a bit that is not piled on top of her head. It is combed so that it goes across her forehead.

The people in the theatre clap after everything she says.

When she says the names of the people who made the films, the people who made the films stand up. They are all in the theatre. When they stand up everyone claps. When they sit down everyone stops clapping. Then Agatha says something else and everyone claps again.

Agatha says Emile's name.

He is sitting in the balcony. He hears his name. He is supposed to stand up. He does not stand up all the way. He stands up enough for Agatha to see him.

She looks on the floor. She does not see Emile. Someone in the balcony sees Emile stand up. He starts clapping. Agatha hears him start clapping.

She looks up. She sees Emile. She points to Emile. Everyone starts clapping.

Emile tries to smile. He sits down.

Everyone stops clapping.

Agatha says the name of another film. Everyone claps. She says the names of the people who made the film. They stand up. Everyone claps again. The people who are standing sit down. Everyone stops clapping.

Agatha reads the name of the last film written on the piece of paper in her hand. There is clapping and people standing up and sitting down and then the clapping stops again.

Agatha puts her hands behind her back.

She says: 'Thank you, everyone, for coming out tonight.'

Everyone claps again. There are some people who shout. Agatha walks back to where she was sitting. The light in front of the screen goes off.

There are curtains over the screen. The curtains open. Everyone stops clapping. The films start playing.

Emile says: 'Don't look.'

Isobel puts her hands over her eyes.

This is not in the movie theatre. It is the room over the grocery store. It is Emile's film.

Isobel is sitting on a bed. It is the bed with plain white sheets. Emile is sitting beside her.

She has her hands over her eyes. Emile stands up.

He says: 'Promise you won't look.'

Isobel says: 'I won't.'

It is summer. The window is open. Emile's and Isobel's feet are bare.

Emile walks to a corner of the room.

There is a suitcase in the corner. Beside it there is a knapsack. They are both on the floor. Beside the knapsack there is a pile of clothes. They are Emile's clothes.

Emile opens the suitcase. He reaches inside the suitcase. He does something with his hands inside the suitcase and then he lifts them up into the air. He is moving carefully. There are strings hanging from his fingers.

A girl climbs out of the suitcase. She is not really a girl. She is too small. She fits inside a suitcase. She is made of wood.

She climbs out of the suitcase and she stands on the floor. She turns her head like she is looking around the room. It is like she is looking for something.

She starts to walk. She puts one of her feet in front of her other foot. She moves clumsily. She takes a step. She takes another step.

She is walking towards Isobel.

Emile says: 'Open your eyes.'

Emile is kneeling in the middle of the room. Isobel opens her eyes. She sees him. His body is bent over the girl standing on the floor. Isobel looks at Emile and then she looks at the girl standing on the floor in front of him.

The girl stops moving.

She stops moving because there is someone looking at her. It is like she is shy. She looks down at the floor. She stands still. Isobel looks at her. Isobel makes a small sound. The girl looks up at her.

Isobel says: 'Is that my hair?'

The girl has thick black hair. It hangs down her back to her waist. Her eyes are made from dark glass beads.

Emile says: 'It is.' He says: 'This is you.'

Isobel says: 'Oh.'

She looks at the girl again. The girl looks up at her. Isobel smiles.

Isobel says: 'I like her.'

Emile says: 'She wants to say something.'

Isobel says: 'She does?'

Emile says: 'She does.'

The girl moves her hands to touch her hair. She moves it so that it is not in her face. She moves her hands over her dress. She makes it look neat. She holds her hands in front of her.

Emile looks at Isobel. He says: 'Say something.'

Isobel says: 'I don't have anything to say.'

The girl holds her hands in front of her. Her hands move like she is rubbing them together. It is like she is impatient.

She is looking up at Isobel.

Isobel says: 'No.' She says: 'That's not it.' She pauses. Then she says: 'I have something to say. I'm not going to say it.'

It is like the girl is speaking now. She is not speaking. She is only a puppet. She cannot speak. Isobel is speaking. The puppet moves like she is the one speaking.

Isobel says: 'I don't want to say it.'

The girl's face is pale. She looks away, like she is struggling to find the right words.

Isobel says: 'I won't.'

The girl is wearing a black dress. It is made from a tattered old cloth Emile found. It is belted with a piece of string. Under the dress her legs are bare.

Isobel says: 'I woke up this morning.' The girl is still looking away. It is like she is afraid of what she is saying.

She says: 'I woke up this morning and I was happy. It's not much, to say that I was happy. It's not enough. But what I have to say does not make me happy.'   ·

71

She is not afraid of what she is saying. She is looking away because it is hard to say it. She has to concentrate.

She says: 'I woke up this morning. You were already downstairs. You were having coffee with Mr. Koch and waiting for the delivery truck to come.'

Her voice changes. She is speaking differently. It is like it is not hard anymore.

She says: 'I wasn't ready to get up when you got up. I felt you get out of the bed and I pulled the blanket closer to me.'

She settles into what she is saying. It is like she is drifting away into it. She is still looking away. It is a different kind of looking away.

She says: 'And then I woke up. I sat up in the bed. I pulled my hands through my hair.'

She says: 'It didn't do much. But I like the feel of my hands in my hair. I like how it feels when I pull it.'

She reaches her hand up to touch her hair. Her fingers touch it lightly. It is like she does not realize that she is touching her hair.

She says: 'I got out of bed. I walked over to the sink. I filled it with water.'

She says: 'I washed my face.'

She says: 'I washed my face and then I emptied the sink. I watched the water carry my sleep away.'

She says: 'And I stood there.'

She realizes that she is touching her hair. She drops her hand. Her arms are by her sides now.

She says: 'I could see the door in the mirror.'

She says: 'I was standing there. I was naked.'

The girl is not looking away. She is not looking at anything. She is standing straight and tall.

She says: 'I wanted to see you come into the room. I wanted to see my face when I saw you.'

It is like she is being drawn up into what she is saying.

She says: 'I was happy.'

The film ends.

The theatre is dark. Everyone claps their hands in the dark. The next film starts. The clapping stops.

Emile does not want to be sitting beside people he does not know. He stands up. His hands are trembling slightly. He does not want his hands to be trembling. He tries to hold them still. He says: 'Excuse me.'

He leaves the theatre.

Nicolas is working at the bar.

He is wearing a white shirt. He is not wearing a tie. His shirt is open at the collar. It is that kind of a bar. He is wearing his apron around his waist. He is pouring a pint of beer for a woman standing at the bar.

She is wearing a dress and the jacket she wore to the place where she works. She is wearing glasses.

She looks tired.

Someone comes into the bar. Nicolas looks up from pouring the beer. He sees Emile. Emile is walking towards the bar. He is undoing the buttons on his jacket.

Nicolas and Emile nod to each other. Emile takes his cap off. It is cold outside. Nicolas finishes pouring the beer. He puts the glass on the bar.

The woman puts some money on the bar. Nicolas takes the money. He puts it in the cash register behind the bar. She takes the glass of beer. She walks away from the bar.

Emile sits at the bar. He sits with his hands in his lap. Nicolas comes over to him. Nicolas says: 'Is it over already?'

Nicolas could not go to the theatre because he is working at the bar.

Emile says: 'Probably not.'

Nicolas frowns. He says: 'How did it go?'

Emile shrugs. He says: 'It was good.'

Nicolas makes a gin and tonic for Emile. He puts it on the bar. It is in front of Emile. Emile reaches to take some money out of his pocket. Nicolas moves his hand to say that he does not have to.

Emile puts his hands on the bar. He moves the gin and tonic closer to him. He smiles at Nicolas.

Nicolas waits for him to say more. Emile looks into his drink.

Nicolas says: 'Come on. Say something, Emile.'

Emile picks up his glass. He takes a drink. He puts the glass down again.

He shrugs.

He says: 'I do not know what to say.'

Emile picks up his glass. There is ice in it. He taps the side of the glass. The ice settles. It makes a sound when it does.

Emile taps the glass again. The ice does not settle. There is no sound. He wanted there to be a sound. He is slumped at the bar. There are not many people in the bar. They are in small groups. They drink. They talk to each other. It is a quiet night.

Emile wanted something to happen at the theatre. He does not know what.

There is a jukebox in the bar. It is playing a song. Emile drinks from his glass. He puts the glass down on the bar. He looks into the glass.

Nicolas does not say anything. He stands with his elbows resting on the bar. He waits.

Emile says: 'I think it was good.' He says: 'I think that they liked it.'

The song that is playing on the jukebox is a nice song. It is a song that Emile and Nicolas like. Emile does not say anything more. Nicolas does not say anything.

They listen to the song.

Emile finishes his drink. Nicolas makes him another gin and tonic. The song finishes playing. Another song starts. It is not as nice as the other song.

Nicolas takes some coins out of his apron. He gives them to Emile. He says: 'Go do something about the music.'

Emile stands up. He walks over to the jukebox. He has the coins from Nicolas in his hand. He puts them into the jukebox. He picks some songs to play.

He goes back to the bar.

There is someone talking to Nicolas. He is drunk. His words are slurred. He is trying to explain something. It is hard to understand what he is saying. Nicolas looks over to Emile. Nicolas shrugs. He is the bartender. There are things he has to do.

Emile nods his head. He sits down at the bar. His glass is in front of him. There is a drop of water forming on the side of his glass. He picks the glass up. He drinks.

The song that was playing on the jukebox stops playing. It is over. Another song starts to play.

Nicolas listens to the man try to explain something. It has something to do with his business. Emile takes a drink from his glass.

It is late at night. There are still not many people in the bar. Some of the tables are empty. Two of the waitresses are standing at the end of the bar. They are talking to each other.

Emile puts his glass down on the bar. He looks at it.

The man talking to Nicolas finishes trying to explain something. He stands up. He says good night to Nicolas. Then he says good night to anyone else who might hear him say good night. He reaches for his jacket. It is lying on one of the stools at the bar. He puts his jacket on.

It is time for the bar to close.

Emile stands up. He puts his jacket and his cap on. He goes outside.

He stands in the street outside the bar. He takes some tobacco out of his pocket. He makes a cigarette. He does not light it.

He waits for Nicolas.

There are people who were inside the bar standing outside the bar. They are waiting for streetcars and taxi cabs to come. Some of them are getting ready to walk. The man who was trying to explain something is still trying to explain something. He is trying to explain it to someone else now.

No one looks at Emile. No one ever looks at Emile. He is standing away from everyone else. His collar is turned up. It is getting cold at night. He looks in the window. He watches what is happening inside the bar.

The people who work in the bar do the things that they do when the bar closes. Emile watches someone mop the floor. Someone else is in the kitchen washing glasses. When they are done Nicolas comes out of the bar. He is wearing his fancy scarf.

Emile lights his cigarette. He passes it to Nicolas.

Nicolas smokes some of the cigarette. He passes it back to Emile. He says: 'Shall we go?'

Emile nods his head.

They walk to the end of the street. They stop. They wait for a streetcar. They pass the cigarette back and forth between them.

Nicolas has the cigarette. He draws on it. He looks at Emile.

He says: 'There's something bothering you.'

Emile shrugs his shoulders. Nicolas passes the cigarette to him. Emile takes the cigarette. He draws on it.

Emile says: 'I do not know what I am going to do.'

Nicolas punches him in the shoulder. He does it playfully. He says: 'You'll think of something.'

The streetcar comes.

They get on the streetcar. They go home.

❧ 6 ❧

Isobel is not asleep.

She is lying in her bed. There is a blanket over her. It is the middle of the night. She is looking up at the ceiling.

Light is coming in through the window. There is a light in the alley. It is coming in through the window. Isobel can see it on the ceiling.

She watches the light on the ceiling. She is not asleep. She wants to be asleep but she is not asleep. She tried to go to sleep. Now she is watching the light on the ceiling.

There is nothing else to do.

She sits up.

She holds the blanket to her body. It is cold in the room. It cannot be helped. It is cold outside.

She pulls her hands through her hair. She wants to sleep. It does not matter that she will have nightmares. She is tired. She needs to sleep. She does not understand why she is not sleeping.

She stands up.

She is naked. Goosebumps rise on her skin. She shivers. She is thin. She gets cold easily. She walks to the middle of the room.

When she walks she looks clumsy. She is too tall. Her body is too long.

She is standing in the middle of the room. The light is over her head. She pulls on the cord hanging from the light. The light turns on.

She pulls her hands through her hair. Her hair is long and thick and almost black. When she is naked it looks like she has too much hair. It looks too heavy hanging from her head.

Her dress is on the floor by the bed. She walks over to where her dress is. She bends down. She picks it up. She puts it on the bed. She looks at her dress lying on her bed.

It is dirty. The collar is ripped. It is coming off the dress. She scowls. She is tired of wearing this dress. She puts it on.

She raises her dress over her head and lets it fall onto her body. It is supposed to be a nice dress. It has frills at the collar. It shows her collarbones. It is not warm. There are still goose-bumps on her skin.

She walks to the door. Her shoes are beside the door. She puts her shoes on. She opens the door. She pulls her hands through her hair again. She ties her hair back.

She leaves the room.

She is standing in the street. She is in front of the grocery store. It is not dark. The street lights are on. It would be dark if the street lights were not on. It is the middle of the night.

Isobel is standing in the street.

She wants to go somewhere. She is standing in the street in the middle of the night. She does not know where she can go. She knows where she can go during the day but she does not know where to go at night. She has never been allowed to stay out this late before.

She wraps her arms around her body. It is cold. She does not know if there is anywhere to go.

She wants there to be somewhere to go.

She stands in front of the grocery store. She looks up and down the street. Both directions look the same in the dark. She walks down the street. It does not matter which way she goes. She does not know what the difference would be.

She walks down the street. She looks for a place where the lights are still on. The street lights are on. The buildings she walks past do not have their lights on. They are dark. Her arms are wrapped around her body. She is cold.

She walks from one street light to the next street light.

There is a pub still open. It is on a street off the main street. Isobel sees the light coming from inside the pub. It is late. The pub will close soon. The people left in the pub are sitting in front of their drinks.

They are drinking. They do not speak. They do not want to speak. They are drinking.

Isobel walks down the street the pub is on. She stops in front of the pub. The lights inside are still on. She looks into the pub. She sees the people inside the pub. She sees them drinking.

She stands in front of the pub. She does not go into the pub. She looks into the pub but she does not go into it.

She wants to go into the pub.

She has never been in a pub before. She does not know if she should.

The people inside wrap their hands around their drinks. They lift their drinks to their mouths and then they put their drinks down. They do not let go of their drinks. They are hunched over and they keep their hands wrapped around their drinks. It is like they are afraid their drinks will be taken away from them.

Some of them are smoking cigarettes. They hold their cigarettes in one hand and they hold their drinks in their other hand.

They drink with one hand and they smoke with the other hand.

They do not look at each other. They do not want to. They are drinking. Their eyes do not leave their drinks.

Isobel stands outside the pub. She is under a street light. She looks into the pub. Someone gets up to leave. He goes towards the door and then he stands in the door. He looks at Isobel.

He looks at her dress. It is not a warm dress. The front is cut low. He can see her breasts.

The man standing in the doorway smiles. It is an ugly smile.

Isobel looks at him. She does not smile. She crosses her arms in front of her. She scowls.

The man shrugs his shoulders. He steadies himself in the doorway. He steadies himself and then he walks away from the bar.

Isobel watches him walk away from the bar. He is wearing a shabby old jacket. There is a rip in one of the shoulders. There is stuffing coming out of it. His hands are in the pockets of his jacket. It is cold. He walks with his shoulders bent over.

Isobel is not wearing a jacket. Her legs are bare. She does not go into the pub. She watches the man walk away from the pub.

She watches until the man turns a corner.

The pub is closing.

The rest of the men are walking away from the pub. They are wearing jackets. Their jackets are also shabby and old. Their hands are stuffed into the pockets. It is cold. They walk with their shoulders bent over.

They mutter to each other. Their voices are not loud enough to carry. They mutter and they walk from the light of one street light to the light of the next street light. Some of them do not mutter. They are alone. They walk from one street light to the next street light.

Isobel is still standing outside the pub. They walk past her. They look at her when they walk past her. They look at her for too long. They do not smile. They are going to their homes. They are going to go to sleep.

They have to get up in the morning. They need to go to sleep.

Isobel watches the owner of the pub come to the door. She watches him lock it. She watches him move around inside the pub. He is cleaning up. When he is done he turns out the lights.

Isobel walks away from the pub.

She walks slowly. She is not going anywhere. She does not have to walk quickly.

She walks from the light of one street light to the light of another street light. The pub is closed. The only lights left are the street lights.

Isobel is shivering. It is cold. She squeezes her hands under her arms. It does not make her hands warm.

She stops walking. She feels useless. She scowls. She turns around. She walks back to the grocery store.

She goes to the alley behind the grocery store. She has the key to the door that goes into the back of the grocery store. It is in her pocket. She sits down on the steps going up to the door.

She does not want to go inside. She sits on the steps behind the grocery store.

She takes out a pack of cigarettes. She takes a cigarette out. She puts it between her lips. There is a book of matches tucked into the pack of cigarettes. She lights the cigarette.

She draws on it. She blows smoke out of her mouth. There is a light on in the alley. It is over the door going into the back of the grocery store.

Isobel is sitting on the steps behind the grocery store. It is cold out. It is colder than it is inside the grocery store. Isobel does not want to be in the grocery store.

She sits on the steps. Her arms are wrapped around her body. She smokes her cigarette.

She does not want to be here.

She saw her mother today. Her mother came into the grocery store. Isobel was pushing the cart in one of the aisles in the grocery store. Her mother was in the aisle. Her mother saw her pushing a cart in an aisle in the grocery store.

Her mother was carrying a basket. There were things in her mother's basket.

Her mother said: 'Isobel.'

Her mother brought her hand up to her mouth. She was surprised. Isobel stopped pushing the cart. She stood behind it. She looked at her mother.

Her mother reached out to touch Isobel. She put her hand on Isobel's face.

She said: 'Isobel. Come home.'

Isobel did not say anything. She turned around. Her mother said: 'Please come home.' Isobel walked away from her mother. She went to the room at the back of the grocery store. Her mother said: 'Isobel.'

Isobel was in the room at the back of the grocery store. There were tears on her face. She did not want there to be tears on her face. She heard her mother say: 'Isobel!' She said it loudly. Mr. Koch heard her.

Mr. Koch came out of his office. He saw Isobel. He saw tears on Isobel's face. He went into the front of the grocery store. He stood in front of Isobel's mother. They said things to each other.

Isobel did not want to hear the things that they said to each other. She heard the things that they said to each other.

There were tears on her face. She could not stop them.

She has already said the last thing she wants to say to her mother. She said: 'I want to spend the night with him.' She said: 'You cannot stop me. I'm going.'

The tears were hot. They hurt her.

She is sitting on the steps behind a grocery store. She is just a girl. It is the middle of the night. It is cold outside. She is cold. She is smoking a cigarette.

She is here.

Her body hurts. Her body has not hurt like this before. She has not worked like this before. She is dirty. She wears the same dress all the time. She has no reason to keep clean. She does not know how to make her body stop hurting.

She is here because she does not know where else she could be.

She finishes her cigarette.

She stands up. She walks up the steps to the door. She takes the key out of her pocket. She unlocks the door. She goes inside. There are no windows in this room. There is only the light coming in through the door.

Isobel closes the door. It is dark. There are things in the room. She walks through the room. It does not matter that it is dark. She knows where the things in the room are. She walks without bumping into the things in the room.

She goes to the stairs. She opens the door to the room at the top of the stairs. It is not really a room. It is the attic. She goes inside.

It is dark in the room. It is not as dark as it is downstairs. There is a window in the room. There is light from the alley outside coming in. It is not much light. It is still dark in the room.

It is her room.

She walks to the middle of the room. She pulls the cord hanging from the ceiling. The light turns on.

There is a bed in the room. There is a sink on one of the walls. There is a towel hanging on the wall next to the sink.

Isobel walks to the bed. She sits on it. She does not take her dress off. She sits on the bed. She looks at her room.

It is what she has here.

She does not know anywhere else she could be. She is here.

She is sitting on the bed. There is a blanket on the bed. She takes her dress off.

She has to learn to like being here.

It is cold in the room. She shivers. She crawls under the blanket on the bed. She knows she is not going to go to sleep.

There is nothing else to do. She is naked. She crawls under the blanket on the bed. She closes her eyes.

The light from the alley is on the ceiling. The ceiling is made of planks of wood. Isobel has her eyes closed. She does not see the light on the ceiling.

She does not go to sleep.

It is cold. It is not as cold under the blanket. Isobel does not need to have her arms wrapped around her body. She is lying on her back. She is lying with her arms by her sides.

She puts one of her hands between her legs. She closes her eyes tighter. She does not want to be here. She has to learn to cope with being here.

She lets her mouth open. She has one hand between her legs. She presses her legs together. She touches herself with her hand. She is trying to remember what it was like. She is starting to forget what it was like. She touches her mouth with her other hand.

She bites down on her fingers.

She wants it to mean something. She needs it to mean something. She opens her mouth. She closes her eyes tighter. She tilts her head back. Her legs are pressed together. Her mouth opens wider.

She lets her breath out. She is lying on her back. She puts her arms by her sides. She is in a bed. The bed has plain white sheets. She is lying between the sheets. There is a blanket over her.

She curls her legs up against her body.

She does not remember what it was like. She is lying in a bed. She wants to go to sleep. She does not go to sleep.

Her eyes are open. She sees the light from the alley on the ceiling. It is coming in through the window. There are curtains on the window. They are flimsy. The light shines through them.

It is the middle of the night. She looks at the light on the ceiling. It is from the street lights in the alley. It is coming in through the window.

Dear Emile,

I am sitting in your room. I know that it is not your room, you are gone and I am the one who lives here now. I know. But still, I want to say that it's your room. It's ridiculous. I don't ever say that it's your room. It would make Mr. Koch shake his head and sigh. But I want to.

It only makes sense for me to be here if it's your room.

I wake up in the night. I don't sleep well anymore, Emile. I wake up in the night and I'm lying in your bed. This is when it matters most that it's your bed. I'm not entirely awake, but I'm not still asleep either. I am in a place somewhere in between. I can't tell if I'm seeing things or if I'm dreaming them. No, it's not that I can't tell. I can't remember what the difference is.

I want you, Emile. I am lying in your bed and I want you. The blanket lying over me is you. I know that it's not you but I can't remember what the difference is.

I wrap my legs around it and I hold you close to me. I bury my face in your shoulder. I bite down on my lip.

It helps me to sleep. I am tired, Emile. I am always tired. I need to sleep and I can't. I don't know why.

It helps. You help me.

I love you.

≈ 7 ≈

There is a suitcase in Emile's closet.

It is the suitcase he had on the train. The knapsack he had on the train is on the floor. It is empty. Some of the clothes that were in it are put away and some of them are the floor.

It is morning. There is sunlight coming in through the window. There is not much sunlight coming in through the window. The window is too small.

Emile is asleep. He will not be asleep much longer. Nicolas is awake. He is moving around in the kitchen.

Emile hears him. He wakes up. He gets out of bed. He is wearing an undershirt and his underwear. He puts his trousers on. They were on the floor beside his bed. He rubs at his eyes. His hair is sticking up from his head. Emile has unremarkable hair. It is kind of blond. It is always messy.

Emile opens the door to his room. He steps out.

Nicolas sees him come out of his room. He takes two cups out of the cupboard. He puts them on the table. Emile goes over to the table. He sits down. Nicolas pours coffee into the two cups.

Nicolas sits down at the table. He takes one of the cups. Emile takes the other cup. Emile looks into his cup. Nicolas drinks from his.

They do not say anything.

Emile looks into his cup of coffee. He says: 'What happened to your paintings?'

Nicolas drinks from his cup again. He puts it down on the table. It is not early in the morning. The sun is coming in the kitchen window.

Nicolas shakes his head.

He says: 'I don't have the time anymore.'

Emile says: 'What happened to them?'

Nicolas says: 'They're in my closet.'

Emile looks into his cup of coffee. He drinks from it. He does not say anything. Nicolas drinks from his cup.

Nicolas says: 'Are you meeting Agatha today?'

Emile nods his head.

They drink from their cups again.

Nicolas says: 'Do you want to go for breakfast first?'

Emile shrugs his shoulders. Nicolas waits for him to say something. Emile does not say anything. He nods his head again.

Emile and Nicolas sit at the table. They drink from their cups of coffee. When their cups are empty, they put them down on the table.

They stand up.

They leave their cups on the table. They can wash them when they come back. They put their coats on. They leave the apartment.

Emile opens the suitcase.

He is sitting on the floor in his room. It is dark outside. Nicolas is working at the bar. Emile is alone. The suitcase is on the floor in front of him. It is an old suitcase. There are leather straps around it.

He undoes the leather straps around the suitcase. He opens the suitcase.

There is a girl inside it.

She is not the only thing in the suitcase. There are arms and legs and other bodies. They are wrapped in cloth. They are puppets. They are not moving. They are still and silent.

She is lying on her side. Her legs are curled up against her body. The other puppets are lying beside her. They are pressed against her. She is holding her head in her hands.

Her fingers are digging into her hair. She is moving. She is not moving very much. She cannot move very much. There are other bodies pressing against her. She is stirring like she is asleep.

She moves suddenly. She raises her head, like she is awake now. She tries to move her arms and legs but she cannot move her arms and legs. The other bodies are too close to her.

She wriggles. She pushes against them. She puts her feet against the bottom of the suitcase and she pushes herself up.

She is standing.

She sways. It is like she did not think that she could stand up. Her dress is twisted around her body. It is black. It is made from an old scrap of cloth. She moves her hands to straighten it.

She turns her head, like she is looking around.

Emile is there. His hair is sticking up from his head. His clothes are old and tattered. They have been mended. If they had not been mended, they would have fallen apart.

He is standing with his hands together in front of him. He is not really Emile. He is a puppet that looks like Emile.

He is watching her.

She moves her hands over her dress. It is the same black dress she wore before. She moves her hands through her hair so that it is not in her face. Her hair is very long. It is not easy to get it so that it is not in her face.

When her hair is not in her face she looks at Emile. He is standing in front of her. He is watching her. She looks at Emile and then she turns her head to look past him.

She is standing in Emile's room. She did not know that she was in Emile's room. She had been inside the suitcase. Emile is standing in front of her. She does not look at him. She looks around the room.

Emile says: 'I am here now.'

She stops looking around the room. She looks where Emile is standing. He is standing in front of the open suitcase. She is still standing inside it. She tilts her head. It is like she is curious. It is like she is waiting for him to say more.

Emile says: 'I left.'

Before they were in this room Emile said that he was going to go. They were in another room. They were lying on a bed. The bed was made with plain white sheets. She listened when he said: 'I am going to go.'

She said: 'I know.'

Now, she shakes her head. It does not matter anymore. He left. Everything is different. She is standing in the suitcase he had when he left.

Emile says: 'There are things happening.'

She lifts one of her feet up. She puts it down on one of the bundles of cloth around her. She steps onto it. The thing shifts under her. It would moan if it could. She puts her arms out to balance herself. She is closer to where Emile is standing.

He says: 'I want to tell you what's happening.'

She lifts her other foot. She puts it on the edge of the suitcase. She balances on the edge of the suitcase and then she takes a step. She is not in the suitcase anymore. She is standing in the light. It is an electric light. It is the lamp on top of the dresser. She has been in the suitcase. It was dark in the suitcase. She is not used to light. She lifts her hands up to shield her eyes.

In the room over the grocery store, the light had been harsh. It was too bright. The sun came in through the window in the morning and it was too bright.

Isobel would kick the sheets away. She would roll over on top of him and hold his face in the light. He would try to turn away but she would hold him.

He would wake up.

They would sit in the bed together. They would look at each other in the light that was too bright. They could see each other too well.

They did not mind.

The light here is not bright. It is an electric light. It is dim and it flickers and it makes a buzzing sound. The two puppets are standing in the light the lamp makes. They are looking at each other.

There are people going by on the street outside. There is a streetcar coming.

She looks at him standing in front of her. She tilts her head. It is like she is curious. She looks around the room like she knows that there are things happening outside.

Emile says: 'I am not sure what's happening.'

She wants to know what is happening. There are people who have stopped to talk in the street outside. They have deep voices. It sounds like they have thick moustaches. They are talking quickly and heatedly. She can hear them. She does not know what they are saying but she can hear them speaking.

He says: 'I don't know what is going to happen.'

She looks at Emile. She should say something. It is like she knows she should say something. He wants her to.

She does not say anything. There is nothing for her to say.

Emile reaches for her hand. They are standing beside each other. She pulls his hand closer to her. She rests her head on him. He puts his arm around her body.

The wood of their bodies makes a hard sound when they touch.

He says: 'I don't know what I am going to do.'

She burrows her face into his neck. He touches her hair with his hand. He looks up at the ceiling.

Her hair is glued to the top of her head. Under her hair her head is made of wood.

He says: 'I don't know.'

The streetcar has gone. It is late. There are no more sounds coming in through the window.

Emile puts his hands down. There are strings tangled around his fingers. He untangles the strings from his fingers. His body is hunched over. He raises his hands over his head. He stretches his body so that his back straightens.

His body does not straighten all the way. Emile's shoulders are always a bit hunched over. He is kneeling near his bed.

He stands up. He walks over to the corner of the room. There is a camera there. It is on a tripod. He turns it off. It had been making a clicking sound. It stops. He turns the lamp on the dresser off. He goes out of his room.

He goes to where his jacket is hanging. It is by the door that goes out of the apartment. He takes his tobacco out of the pocket.

He sits at the table. There are four chairs at the table. He makes a cigarette.

He stands in the doorway to his room. There is light coming in through the window. It is not very much light. It is still dark in his room.

He lights his cigarette. He stands in the doorway to his room. He looks at the two puppets on the floor. He smokes his cigarette.

He goes into the kitchen. There is an ashtray on the table there. He puts his cigarette out in the ashtray.

He sits at the table.

It is quiet in the apartment. It is too quiet in the apartment. He does not want to sit at the table.

He stands up. He goes to the door. He puts his jacket on and then he puts his shoes on. He puts his cap on his head.

He leaves the apartment.

He goes out the door. He locks it behind him. He goes down the stairs. He goes out the door that goes to the street. He closes the door behind him. He goes to where the streetcar stops. He stands there until a streetcar comes.

It is the middle of the night. It is cold. He does not have his gloves. They are in the apartment. He did not bring them with him.

He puts his hands into the pockets of his coat.

A streetcar comes. Emile gets on the streetcar. He pays his fare. The driver gives him a ticket. Emile finds a place to sit. The streetcar moves. It stops and then it moves again. It stops and then Emile gets off the streetcar.

He walks down the street. There is no one walking on the street. There is a homeless man lying in a doorway. He has blankets and newspapers on him. He is asleep.

Emile is in front of the bar. He stops. He tries to open the door. It does not open. It is locked.

He looks in the window. Nicolas is inside the bar. Emile knocks on the glass. Nicolas looks at the window. He sees Emile standing outside the bar.

Nicolas opens the door.

Nicolas says: 'Emile.' He says: 'What're you doing out?'

Emile says: 'Can I come in?'

Nicolas says: 'Of course.'

He holds the door open for Emile. Emile goes into the bar.

Nicolas had been mopping the floor. There is a bucket in the middle of the floor with a mop standing in it.

Emile and Nicolas walk to the bar. All of the stools are upside down on top of the bar. Nicolas takes two stools down. He puts them on the floor.

Emile sits down on one of the stools. He sits so that his back is to the bar. He looks out into the room.

There is no one else in the bar. There is no one walking past on the street outside. It is too late for that.

Nicolas goes behind the bar. He gets two glasses. He pours gin and tonic into them. He comes out from behind the bar. He is carrying the two glasses.

Nicolas sits down next to Emile. He gives Emile one of the glasses.

Nicolas says: 'Were you working?'

Emile takes a sip from his glass. He nods his head.

Nicolas say: 'How is it going?'

Emile does not say anything. He drinks from his glass. He looks into the empty room. He does not say anything. Nicolas does not say anything. He looks at Emile. He waits.

Emile says: 'I am not sure.'

They sit at the bar. There is no one else in the bar. They look into the empty room.

Emile says: 'I do not know what it is.' He drinks from his glass. He says: 'I do not know if there is anything to it.'

He does not say anything more. Nicolas nods his head.

Emile is still wearing his jacket. Nicolas is wearing a white shirt. It is open at the collar. The sleeves are rolled up. His shoes were carefully polished. He worked all night. They are not as carefully polished now.

They finish their drinks.

Nicolas says: 'I need to finish mopping.'

Emile nods his head.

They stand up. Emile takes the two empty glasses behind the bar. He washes them. Nicolas mops the floor.

When Nicolas is done mopping the floor he gets his jacket and his fancy scarf. They leave the bar. They go to the corner where the streetcar stops.

They wait for a streetcar to come.

A streetcar comes. They get on. The streetcar moves and then they get off the streetcar.

They are standing on the platform in the middle of the street. They cross the street to the sidewalk. They walk down the street. They go to the door to their apartment.

Nicolas takes his key out of his pocket. He opens the door. They go inside and up the stairs. They go into their apartment. They take their jackets and their shoes off. Nicolas takes his scarf off and Emile hangs his cap on a hook.

Emile goes to the table in the kitchen. He sits down. He starts to make a cigarette.

Nicolas shakes his head. He says: 'I'm tired, Emile.'

Emile nods his head. He puts his tobacco away.

Nicolas goes into his room. He closes the door behind him. Emile is still sitting at the table.

There is a bowl in the middle of the table. There are apples and oranges in the bowl.

Some of the apples and oranges are bruised.

Emile sits at the table. His shoulders are hunched forward. He looks at the apples and oranges in the bowl. He rubs at his eyes.

He stands up. He stands beside the table for a moment. He goes over to where the light switch is. He turns the lights out. He goes into his room.

He closes the door behind him.

Dear Emile,

You were on the train.

It's what I remember most vividly. How I stood on the platform and watched you get on the train. You walked down the aisle, awkwardly, because you were carrying your things, and then you sat down.

You looked out the window. You saw me.

I made sure that my hair was not in my face, I smoothed the front of my dress and I stood with my hands held together in front of me. I did not cry because I wanted to be strong. I wanted you to have that to take away with you.

You saw me and you smiled.

And then you were gone. I was left standing there, with just the image of the train vanishing in the distance.

I was not sure what I would do.

I remembered being on the train when I was a little girl. I was going somewhere with my mother. I don't remember where but wherever it was it was important at the time. I remember there was an old woman sitting across from me. She smelled sour and I didn't like her. It was the way that she looked at me. I didn't like it. I was sitting on my mother's lap with my face pressed up against the window. I looked out and I wanted everything that went past. I wanted it so fiercely. I would have wriggled off my mother's lap and reached out the window as far as I could, I would have grabbed everything that went rushing past, but I couldn't. The windows didn't open. I could only look.

I don't know where you are, Emile. I don't know what you are doing. I imagined you sitting on the train with your things in your lap. You would have wanted them close to you, so you could be sure that they were safe.

And I imagined you looking out the window.

I'm sitting on your bed now. It is late, I should be getting ready to go to sleep, but I am just sitting here. My dress is lying on the floor. I'm naked. I'm looking at myself in the mirror, at the places you touched me. I try to touch myself like you touched me. I'm trying to remember the way that your hands moved, and what it was like to feel your hands move, and I can't. I can't do it.

It is getting cold here, especially at night. I am shivering. I should get into bed, I should go to sleep. I don't want to.

I don't want to be in this place. I don't want to be the kind of person who lives in this place. But I am. You are what makes me more than this. The way that you touched me, what it left behind in my body. I touch myself to remember what we were. To keep it alive.

I want more, Emile. I want what you saw, when you looked out the window of the train. I want what I saw. Sometimes I remember what it is like to want so fiercely. And sometimes I am just a girl lying in bed touching myself.

You saw me standing on the platform. You saw how strong I am. You know what I can be. I need to know that you saw that. I'm not sure that I can do it, sometimes, and I need to remember that you saw me. It's so that I do not forget.

I am a girl living in a room over a grocery store. I don't want this. I want my body to be electric and alive, not this sad, worn-out thing. I want to be more than this. I have to be.

I love you, Emile.

Isobel is in the room over the grocery store.

It is late. When it was earlier she was working in the store. It is late now. She is not working. Mr. Koch has gone. He stood at the bottom of the stairs. He said: 'Good night, Isobel.' He left.

Isobel is alone.

Her body hurts. She does not notice that her body hurts anymore. She is used to it. She has been here long enough that she is used to it. It still hurts. She sits on the bed. She rubs her shoulders and her arms with her hands. It helps.

Her dress is dirty. It is starting to smell. She touches her side. There is a rip in her dress there. It is under her arm. She tried to mend it. It did not work. The cloth is too worn.

She takes her dress off. She drops it onto the floor. She stands up.

She stands in the middle of the room. She looks at the mirror. She is not as thin as she was. Her body is harder. She is getting stronger. She did not think she would change like this. It is a relief. It is not how she wants to change. It is a relief to see that she can change.

She is in the room over the grocery store. She is standing under the light. She reaches up. She turns the light out. She walks over to the bed.

She is tired. She is always tired. She does not sleep well. There is nothing she can do about it. She gets into bed. She is naked. She curls her legs up against her body. She puts her hands between her legs. It is warmer with her hands between her legs.

There is light coming in through the window. It is from the street lights outside. Isobel closes her eyes. She is cold. It cannot be helped. It is cold in the room. If she lies under the blanket for long enough then she will be warmer.

She is shivering. She pulls her legs tighter against her body. She keeps her eyes closed.

It is later. Isobel is asleep.

She is lying with the blanket tangled around her. She is holding part of it with her hands. Another part of it is between her legs.

She is moving in her sleep. She is squeezing her legs together.

It is cold in the room. It cannot be helped. It is cold outside. Isobel is moving in her sleep. The blanket is tangled around her. It is tangled so that it is not covering her.

She is naked. There are goosebumps on her skin.

She tries to stay asleep. She is dreaming. She is dreaming that she is cold.

She pulls on the blanket. It moves between her legs.

She is standing in a room. There are white tiles on the floor and on the walls and on the ceiling of the room. There is a bathtub in the room. It is in the middle of the room.

She is naked. She is walking towards the bathtub. She is going to take a bath.

She sits on the edge of the bathtub. She puts her legs into the tub. The water comes up to her knees. She puts her hands on the edges of the tub. She lowers herself into the water.

She is curled up on the bed. She shivers.

The water in the bathtub is cold. She shivers. Her hair is floating on the water. She moves her hands under the water. It does not feel pleasant.

The water is dirty. It does not bother her.

She thinks for a moment that it should bother her. She does not know why it should bother her. She decides she does not mind.

She closes her eyes. She lets her head go under the water. Her hair is floating around her head. It is like seaweed in the ocean.

She opens her eyes. The water is cold. There are goosebumps on her skin. It does not bother her. She likes it. The water is filthy. It is grey. There are things floating in it. She closes her eyes.

She raises her head. It is not under the water anymore. She lets her breath out. She moves so she is sitting.

Her back is against the edge of the tub. It is not comfortable. The bathtub is not big enough. She cannot straighten her legs. Her knees stick up out of the water.

She rests her head on the edge of the bathtub. She lets her mouth open. Her hair is over her face. It is tangled around her shoulders and floats on the surface of the water. She is cold. She can feel her skin shrivelling. She can feel herself starting to sleep.

Her mother is here.

She cannot hear her but there is something in the room that is different. She cannot say what it is. She knows that her mother is here.

She opens her eyes. Her mother is standing in the room. Isobel lifts her head. She puts her hands on the edge of the tub. She lifts her body out of the water.

She stands up. She is standing in the tub. Water runs off her body. She is filthy. Her hair is filthy. It is tangled and matted and clings to her body.

Her mother looks at her.

Isobel does not want to be naked. She tries to cover her body. She uses her hands.

Her hands do not cover her body. She is filthy.

Her mother can see her naked.

She turns her head away. Her nipples are hard from the cold. She can feel them. She puts her hands between her legs. She does not want her mother to see her. She is going to cry. She closes her eyes. She does not want to cry.

She wakes up. She is lying in her bed. The blanket is tangled around her body. She is going to cry. She does not want to cry.

She holds her breath and she closes her eyes. It stops her from crying.

She moved while she was dreaming. She is more tangled up in the blanket than she was before. She has to untangle the blanket from her body.

She could have stepped out of the tub. She did not.

She untangles the blanket from her body. She sits up in the bed. She pulls her hands through her hair. Her hands are shaking.

She is cold. She cannot help it. It is cold in the room.

She pulls her hands through her hair. Her hair is wet. Her dream made her sweat. Her skin is clammy. She straightens the blanket on the bed. It is the middle of the night. The light from the alley is coming in through the window.

It is dark in the room. It is dark and it is cold.

Isobel stands up. She walks over to the sink. She turns the water on. She puts some water on her face. The water is clean.

She cannot see her face in the mirror. It is dark in the room. She starts to shiver. She is glad she cannot see her face in the mirror. She does not want to know what she looks like now.

She turns the water off. She walks back to the bed.

She sits on the bed. She pulls her knees up against her body. She wraps her arms around her legs. It is the middle of the night. There is nothing else to do.

She lies down on the bed. She pulls the blanket over her. She closes her eyes.

She does not go to sleep.

She sits up in the bed. She pushes the blanket away. She stands up. She turns the light on.

She goes back to the bed. She does not sit down on it. She reaches under it. There is a notebook under the bed. It is a coil notebook. There is a pencil tucked in the coils.

She writes letters in the notebook. She takes it out from under the bed. She takes the blanket off the bed. She wraps the blanket around her body. She sits down on the bed.

She opens the notebook. The paper in it is yellow. It is thin and flimsy. It has blue lines on it. She reads what she wrote before.

She pulls her hands through her hair. She writes. She is tired. She writes until she is too tired to write anymore.

She closes the notebook. She tucks the pencil into the coils. She puts it back under the bed. It is where it was before.

There are envelopes beside the notebook. There are letters in the envelopes. They are ready to be sent. They have not been sent. Isobel does not want to send them.

She does not know why.

The blanket is still wrapped around her body. She pulls it closer to her. She lies down on the bed. She rubs at her eyes. She is tired. She does not want to be tired. She does not want to sleep.

She does not want to dream again.

It is not as dark as it was. The night is almost over.

Isobel goes to sleep.

There is light coming in through the window. It is not the light that was coming in from the alley. It is sunlight. It is morning.

Isobel sits up in the bed. She rubs at her face. She is awake. She does not feel awake. She is tired.

She pushes the blanket off her body. Under the blanket she is naked. Her skin is still clammy. She does not care that she is naked. She is too tired.

Oskar will be here soon. He will have his truck. There will be crates to unload.

There is sunlight coming into the room.

She pulls her hands through her hair. Her hair is tangled. It is matted with sweat. She pulls her hands through her hair until it is less tangled.

She sits up in the bed. She swings her legs out of the bed. She is sitting so that she is on the edge of the bed.

It is still cold. She wraps her arms around her body. There are goosebumps on her skin.

There is a sink on the wall. There is a towel hanging next to the sink and there is a curtain over the window. They are flimsy and dirty. Her clothes and her shoes are on the floor.

She stands up. She walks over to the sink. She does not walk steadily. Her body is groggy. She does not sleep well. She is still tired.

She is standing in front of the sink. She turns the water on.

She waits until the water fills the sink. She turns the water off. She washes her face. She washes under her arms and between her legs. She dries herself.

She dries herself with the towel. She stands in front of the sink. She looks at herself in the mirror over the sink.

She is tired. It does not matter that she just slept. Her skin is sallow.

She scowls.

Her dress is on the floor. She goes over to where it is. She picks it up off the floor. It was a nice dress. It has frills around the neck. It is dirty and wrinkled. She does not care. She puts it on.

She goes to the door. She goes out of the room. She goes down the stairs. She is in the room at the back of the grocery store.

She is tired of this. She does not know what to do. She will do something. She does not know what she can do.

She sits down on a crate. She waits for Mr. Koch to come. He will make coffee. He will sit down on a crate. He will give Isobel a cup of coffee.

She picks at her fingernails. She waits.

She is tired of waiting.

Dear Emile,

I am sitting on your bed. I'm the only one who still calls it your bed. You're gone, Emile. What we did is the only reason anyone even remembers you were here. And I am the one who lives here now.

I hate it.

I hate that they say this is my bed.

I'm sitting here, in your room. It's late. I'm tired. I'm always tired now. And I hurt. I'm not used to this, to any of this. My clothes are dirty. I smell. I try to wash myself in the sink and I still smell. I am so tired of this, and all I have to remind myself that there is anything more is a cigarette butt.

The woman at the station dropped it on the platform. It was just after you left, I was still standing on the platform. I watched the train go away and then she was standing there. She looked at me, she finished her cigarette, she dropped it on the ground and then she went back to the ticket booth.

It was the only butt still smoking. I took it. I still have it.

I have to keep it because I don't remember you anymore. Not like I used to. The image of you isn't vivid anymore. I don't remember what your breathing is like, the feel of your hair or the way you hold things in your hands. I try and all that is there is me, sitting on this bed, in this room.

I hold the cigarette butt in my hand. It is all that I have. I have to love it. It's supposed to help me remember but it's just a cigarette butt. It doesn't.

This is stupid.

I want to watch you again, Emile. I want to sit here with my legs curled up under me. I want to watch you working.

You sat on the floor with your puppets. You had their strings in your hands and the way that you held your hands up in the air looked so stupid. And you didn't care. You had to do it, to make them move. That was what mattered to you.

They were bits of wood tied together with string. You painted faces on them and dressed them up in clothes but they were still just bits of wood tied together with string.

And you made them move.

I remember before I knew you. I had heard about you. The strange boy from the city. No one knew what you were doing here. There were rumours, there were so many rumours, but no one knew.

I wanted to know.

I wasn't supposed to see you. You told Mr. Koch that you did not want to be disturbed and he did his best to keep you from being disturbed. I snuck up the stairs when the store was busy.

You'd left your door open.

It was summer and hot out, you needed to leave your door open.

I crept up the stairs and I looked into your room. I stood with my hands against the door frame and one eye peeping in at you.

You were sitting in the middle of the room with your puppets. You had one dangling from each hand. They were moving. I had never seen anything like it before. They were just puppets. They shouldn't have been anything special. But I had never really seen puppets before. Not standing right in front of me, moving.

I laughed.

You heard me and you stopped. I didn't want you to stop. I didn't want you to drop the puppets. It was horrible to see them go limp. It was like they were dead. I said, Please. Don't stop. You wouldn't look at me. You looked like you wanted to hide.

I said, Please.

One of the puppets jerked its head. It started to stand up. It bent down to help the other one. I laughed again. I stood in the doorway and I clapped my hands and I laughed.

I sat and I watched you until it was dark. I went home and I had to explain where I had been. I lied. And I came back. Again and again, I came back.

You touched me, eventually.

You're just a boy, there's nothing special about you. Nothing. Just that I wanted you. I don't know why I did, I don't know if there was a reason or if it just happened. I don't know if that's enough of a reason. I wanted you. I started to realize that I wanted you. That was all. I wanted to touch you.

I'm trying to remember you. We touched each other. I don't know if it means anything. I want it to. I don't know if that's enough.

I need it to. I'm sitting on your bed now. I need it to mean something. I'm not strong enough, Emile. It's stupid. I feel so stupid. I don't know how long I can do this.

I need to be stronger than this.

I am sitting on your bed. You touched me here. We stood close to each other and you looked at me. I took your hand. I put your hand on my face.

It has to mean something that you touched me. I need to make it mean something. I'm going to go to bed now, Emile. I have to be up early, I need to go to sleep.

I don't want to. I hate the feeling of my body sinking into this place. But I'm so tired. I need to sleep.

Where are you?

❧ 9 ❧

Nicolas and Emile are sitting on a streetcar.

Emile is sitting next to the window. He is looking at the window.

He does not see the things going by. He is not looking at them. There are cracks in the window. He is looking at them.

Nicolas is sitting beside him. He is looking at the people in the streetcar. He is trying to catch someone's eye. He does not care whose. He looks at the other people in the streetcar. He tries to make one of them look at him.

No one in the streetcar wants to look at him. He tries anyway. He thinks it is fun. The other people in the streetcar do not. The streetcar is moving. It rocks from side to side as it moves.

Nicolas and Emile are sitting beside each other. The streetcar is moving. Nicolas taps Emile's leg. Emile looks at Nicolas.

Nicolas says: 'Come on.'

Nicolas stands up. He walks through the streetcar to where the doors are. There are other people standing in the streetcar. Nicolas walks past them. He goes to where the doors are.

Emile follows him. Emile holds on to the backs of the seats as he walks. The streetcar is still moving. He is afraid he will stumble.

The streetcar stops. Nicolas and Emile get off the streetcar.

They are standing on a corner. They walk down the street and then they turn onto another street. They walk down this street.

They stop.

Nicolas looks at Emile. He smiles. He says: 'Are you ready?'

Emile nods his head.

They are standing in front of a door. It is between two shops. On one side is a shop that sells magazines. On the other side is a tailor's shop.

Both of the shops are closed. There are bars over their windows. It is late in the evening. They will be open again in the morning.

There is a doorbell beside the door. Nicolas presses the doorbell. He presses it and then he leans against the door frame.

He puts one of his hands in his pockets. He cannot put his other hand in his pocket. He is carrying something in a paper bag.

Emile's hands are already in his pockets. They stand in front of the door.

They wait.

They hear someone coming down the stairs on the other side of the door. Emile fidgets with his cap. The door opens. Agatha is standing in the doorway.

She says: 'Well. Hello.'

She moves so that she is leaning against the door. She says: 'Come in.'

Nicolas and Emile squeeze past Agatha. She is wearing a red dress. It is a short red dress. Her legs are bare.

Agatha closes the door. Nicolas and Emile are standing with her at the bottom of a staircase.

She touches the small of Emile's back with her hand. She presses there.

She says: 'Come on up, you two.'

Emile moves forward when Agatha touches him. He starts to walk up the stairs. Agatha is behind him. She guides him with her hand.

Nicolas smiles. He shakes his head. He follows them up the stairs.

Agatha's apartment is at the top of the stairs.

Agatha is at the top of the stairs. Nicolas and Emile are standing with her. She smiles to them. It is a wolfish smile. She opens the door. Nicolas and Emile go in.

There are other people in the apartment. There are a lot of other people in the apartment. There is music playing.

Agatha is having a party.

Nicolas and Emile take their jackets off. They look for a place to put them.

They are standing by the door. Someone bumps into Nicolas. She almost spills her drink on him. She says: 'Excuse me.'

Agatha looks at Nicolas and Emile. They are holding their jackets in their hands. They look like they do not know what to do with them. Agatha says: 'Put them in the bedroom.'

She points to where the bedroom is.

Nicolas and Emile go into Agatha's bedroom. It is not a large room. There is a large bed in it. There are coats piled on top of the bed. The room smells like cigarette smoke and Agatha's perfume.

They look around the room. There is a vanity table in the room. It is a table with a mirror on it. Some of Agatha's makeup is still out on the table.

Nicolas puts his coat on the bed and then Emile puts his coat on the bed.

They leave the room.

Agatha is waiting for them. She walks towards them. She sways when she does. She puts her arms around Nicolas's shoulders.

She says: 'Hello, Nicolas.'

Nicolas kisses her on the cheek. She says: 'It's good to see you away from the bar.' She smiles. She says: 'Now, if only we could get you painting again.'

She lets go of Nicolas. She turns towards Emile.

She says: 'Hello, you.'

She reaches towards him. She puts her arms around him. She steps closer to him. She says: 'I haven't seen you in ages.'

She kisses him on the cheek. She puts her cheek close to his mouth. She waits for him to kiss her.

Emile kisses her on the cheek.

She says: 'Have you been keeping busy?'

Emile says: 'Yes.'

She says: 'You must tell me what you've been up to.'

She walks away.

Nicolas and Emile are standing in the door to Agatha's bedroom.

Nicolas is holding a bottle of wine. It was in the paper bag he had with him. There are people standing around them. They are talking. It is loud. Nicolas says: 'Let's find some glasses.'

Nicolas and Emile go towards the kitchen.

The people standing around them are between them and the kitchen. The people are standing very close together. They are talking to each other. Some of them are wearing black. Some of them are dressed in very bright colours. Nicolas and Emile have to squeeze between them.

They squeeze between them. They get to the other side of the room. They go down a hallway. There is a door at the end of the hallway. They go through the door. They are in the kitchen.

There are more people in the kitchen. They are standing. They are dressed like the people in the other room. They are talking to each other.

Nicolas and Emile go to where the kitchen table is. There are glasses and bottles of wine on the table. Some of the glasses are wineglasses and others are ordinary glasses. They are empty.

There is a corkscrew on the table. It is with the glasses. Nicolas picks out two glasses. He opens the bottle of wine he is carrying. He pours wine into the two glasses.

He gives Emile one of the glasses. He takes the other one for himself. He says: 'Cheers.'

Nicolas and Emile touch their glasses together. They move away from the table. They do not move very far. They cannot move very far. There are too many people in the kitchen. They are still standing near the table with the bottles of wine on it.

Agatha is also in the kitchen. She came in while Nicolas was opening the bottle.

She has a glass in her hand. It is half full of something. It is a dark liquid. She is talking to someone. He is wearing a black shirt. There are too many buttons undone on his shirt. He is trying to stand too close to her.

Agatha tips her glass up. She drinks what is left in it. She smiles to the man trying to talk to her. She walks away from him.

She walks over to the table with the bottles of wine on it.

Nicolas and Emile are still standing beside the table with the bottles of wine on it. Agatha leans up against Nicolas. She says: 'Pour me a glass, bartender.'

Nicolas takes her glass. He fills it with wine. He gives it back to her.

She says: 'Emile.' She rests her hand on his arm. She says: 'Tell me what you're working on.'

Emile looks at Nicolas. Nicolas winks at him. He walks away from the table. There are other people in the kitchen. He goes to talk to them.

Agatha plucks at Emile's shirt with her fingers. She says: 'Tell me, Emile.'

Emile is holding on to his glass of wine.

He clears his throat.

He says: 'I have two puppets.' He clears his throat again. He is not looking at Agatha.

He says: 'They are in my bedroom.'

He is holding on to his glass of wine. Agatha leans in closer. She smiles. She has a wolfish smile.

She says: 'And?'

Emile holds on to his glass of wine. He says: 'They are in a room.'

She says: 'And?'

Agatha is wearing a short red dress. There is a pattern embroidered on it. The pattern looks Chinese. The dress has straps that go over her shoulders.

One of the straps falls off her shoulder. It is halfway down her arm.

Agatha does not move it back to where it should be. She is standing close to Emile.

Her shoulder is bare. Emile can see her breasts move when she breathes.

Emile looks into his glass. He says: 'I don't know.' He says: 'They are in a room. That's all.'

Agatha smiles again. She moves closer to Emile. She says: 'I'm sure it'll be brilliant.'

Agatha is almost touching Emile. She stumbles. She grabs Emile's shoulder to steady herself. She is drunk. She is very close to him. She does not take her hand away from his shoulder.

She says: 'It'll be brilliant.'

Emile can smell Agatha's perfume. He holds on to his glass.

Nicolas and Emile are standing on the street. They are outside Agatha's apartment. The party is over. They are on their way home.

There are other people on the street. They are also on their way home.

It is late. The streetcars have stopped for the night.

Nicolas looks down the street. He is wearing a jacket and a scarf. He puts his hands in his pockets. He is looking for a taxi.

He does not see a taxi.

Nicolas says: 'Do you want to walk?'

Emile shrugs.

They turn their collars up. It is cold out. Emile takes his tobacco out of his pocket. He rolls a cigarette and he lights it. He passes it to Nicolas.

Nicolas takes it. He smokes some of it. He passes it back to Emile.

Emile smokes some of the cigarette.

Nicolas says: 'What were you and Agatha talking about?'

Emile shrugs. He says: 'She asked me what I am working on.'

Nicolas says: 'And?'

Emile says: 'I told her what I am working on.'

Nicolas looks at Emile. He waits for him to say more.

Emile says: 'That was all.'

He smokes a bit more of the cigarette. He passes it back to Nicolas. Nicolas is smiling at him.

Nicolas says: 'You're sure that was all you talked about?'

Emile says: 'It was.'

Nicolas is still smiling at him.

Emile looks away.

Nicolas smokes some of the cigarette. He passes it back to Emile. Emile finishes the cigarette. He drops it in the gutter.

They are walking down a street with houses on either side of it. There is no one else on the street. There is no one else awake. The street lights are on. There is garbage out on the streets. Trucks will come to take it away in the morning.

Nicolas and Emile are still a long way from home.

Nicolas says: 'Have you heard from that girl you met?'

Emile says: 'Her name is Isobel.'

Emile puts his hands in his pockets. It is cold. They come to the end of the block. They cross the street.

Emile sighs. He says: 'No.'

Nicolas and Emile walk up the stairs to their apartment. They stand in front of the door. Nicolas takes his keys out of his pocket.

He opens the door.

They go inside. Nicolas turns on the light. They take their jackets off. They hang their jackets up. There are hooks on the wall. They hang their jackets on the hooks.

Emile stands by the door. He is tired. He does not want to go to bed.

He sits down at the table.

Nicolas takes two glasses out of the cupboard. He fills them with water. He puts one down in front of Emile and then he sits down across from Emile.

Emile picks up the glass. He drinks some of the water. He puts the glass back on the table.

Nicolas sits down at the table. He is sitting across from Emile. He drinks from his glass of water.

He waits for Emile to say something.

Emile does not speak.

Nicolas drinks from his glass of water. He puts it down on the table. It is empty.

Emile does not say anything. Nicolas shrugs.

He says: 'I'm off to bed.'

He stands up. He goes into his room.

Emile sits at the table. The bowl of fruit is in the middle of the table. Emile's glass is on the table in front of him. The glass is not empty. The bowl of fruit is. Nicolas threw out the bruised fruit two days ago.

Emile sits at the table.

He wanted to say something. He did not know how to say it. If Nicolas had waited longer he might have said it.

He might not have said it.

Emile stands up. He takes the two glasses from the table. He puts them into the sink.

He goes into his room.

There is a dresser against one of the walls. It is where he should be keeping his clothes. His clothes are on the floor. There is a window on one of the walls. It does not have a curtain over it. There is light from the street coming in through the window.

It is enough light to see by.

His bed is in a corner. There are two puppets lying on the bed.

They are lying with their arms around each other and their legs together.

Emile picks the puppets up. Their arms and their legs dangle. He takes them over to the window. He props them up on the windowsill.

They are sitting opposite each other. Their heads are lolling. Emile adjusts their heads so that they are looking into the room.

Emile goes back to the bed. He sits down on it. He takes his clothes off. He drops them on the floor.

He puts his hands in his lap.

He sits on his bed. He looks at the puppets on the windowsill. He looks at them like he is waiting for them to do something.

They do not do something.

Emile sighs. He gets into his bed. He goes to sleep.

Isobel is in the room at the back of the grocery store. There is no one here. It is early in the morning. It is before anyone is here. She goes to the door that goes outside. She opens it.

There is a brick that Mr. Koch leaves beside the door. She props the door open with it.

She goes outside.

It is early in the morning. It is cold out. Isobel does up the buttons on her sweater. She is wearing a sweater. It is new. She is not cold.

She is carrying a pack of cigarettes. It is in her hand. She takes a cigarette out of the pack.

She puts the cigarette between her lips. She lights it with a match.

She shakes the match out. She draws on the cigarette.

She looks down the alley. There is no one in the alley. It is too early. The light is too bright. It is always too bright this early in the morning.

She sits down on the steps. She puts the cigarette between her lips. She draws on it. She exhales. She shifts so that she is more comfortable sitting on the steps.

She looks like she is looking at something. She is not looking at something. There is nothing in the alley to look at.

She is sitting on the steps at the back of the grocery store. She is smoking a cigarette. She is waiting.

That is all.

There is a noise in the store behind her. A door opens and closes. Mr. Koch is here.

She draws on her cigarette. She exhales. She waits while Mr. Koch walks through the store. She hears him on the steps behind her.

She turns around. She looks up at Mr. Koch.

Mr. Koch is wearing an overcoat and a hat and a scarf. The scarf is wrapped loosely around his neck. He has his keys in his hand.

He smiles. He says: 'Good morning, Isobel.'

Isobel says: 'Good morning, Mr. Koch.'

Mr. Koch goes into his office. He takes off his hat and his scarf and his overcoat. He fills his coffee-making machine with water and ground coffee beans.

Isobel is still sitting on the steps behind the store. She puts her cigarette between her lips. She draws on it. She exhales.

The water dribbles through the coffee machine. Mr. Koch takes off his jacket. He loosens his tie. Mr. Koch always wears a tie to the store. He always loosens it when he arrives. He undoes the top button of his shirt.

Mr. Koch looks at the coffee machine. He wipes his forehead with his handkerchief. The coffee-making machine is not done. Mr. Koch waits for it to be done.

The coffee is done. Mr. Koch pours it into two cups. He takes the two cups and he goes out of his office.

The cups are plain cups. They are not fancy. They are for drinking from.

He goes out to the alley.

Isobel is still sitting on the steps. Mr. Koch is standing behind her. He hands Isobel one of the cups.

She turns around. She takes the cup.

Mr. Koch breathes in deeply. He says: 'It is a good morning.'

Isobel does not speak. She moves her hair with her hand. She nods her head.

Mr. Koch stands on the steps. He drinks from his cup of coffee.

He makes a noise in his throat. He reaches into one of the pockets of his waistcoat. He takes a pack of cigarettes out. He takes a cigarette out of it.

He puts the cigarette in his mouth. He takes a lighter from another pocket and he lights the cigarette. He draws on it. Smoke comes out of his mouth.

He makes a contented noise. It comes from deep in his throat.

He puts his cigarette to his mouth again. He draws on it. He drinks from his cup of coffee.

Mr. Koch says: 'It will be too cold soon.' He says: 'Best enjoy the mornings while we can.'

He drinks from his cup of coffee again.

Isobel flicks her cigarette away. She holds her cup with both hands. She drinks from it.

They have their cups of coffee. They do not say anything. They do not need to say anything. They have their cups of coffee.

Isobel moves her hair with her hand. She moves it so that it is tucked behind her ears. Mr. Koch finishes his cigarette. He flicks the butt of it away.

Mr. Koch says: 'Well.' He says: 'I had best get to work.'

He is holding his cup of coffee. He does not turn to go. He is still standing behind Isobel.

Mr. Koch says: 'Are you all right?'

Isobel turns around. She looks up at Mr. Koch. She smiles for him. She has to try to smile.

She says: 'I am.'

Mr. Koch says: 'Good, good.' He says: 'Well.' He drinks from his cup of coffee. He clears his throat. He says: 'I will see you inside.'

Mr. Koch goes back into the grocery store. He goes into his office.

Isobel stays on the steps behind the store.

She takes another cigarette out of her pack of cigarettes. She puts it between her lips. She lights it.

She waits for Oskar to come with his truck.

Oskar's truck turns into the alley.

Isobel is still sitting on the steps. She is holding her cup of coffee in her hands.

She puts her cup down on the step beside her. She stands up. She stretches her arms up over her head. Oskar sees her. He honks the horn on his truck.

He stops his truck. He stops it so that the back of it is beside the steps going up into the store. He turns the engine off.

He gets out of his truck. He is by the steps that go into the grocery store.

Isobel is waiting for him. Oskar says: 'Good morning, Isobel.'

Isobel says: 'Good morning.'

Oskar smiles. He opens the back of the truck. There are crates in the back of the truck.

Oskar says: 'Will Mr. Koch be out?'

Isobel says: 'He will.'

Oskar gets into the back of the truck. He puts his work gloves on. He hands Isobel one of the crates. Isobel takes the crate. She goes into the grocery store with it. Oskar follows her. He is also carrying a crate.

They put the crates down beside the door.

Mr. Koch hears them come into the store. He comes out of his office.

Mr. Koch says: 'Oskar!' He says: 'I thought I'd heard you drive up.'

Oskar says: 'Good morning, Mr. Koch.'

Mr. Koch says: 'Good morning, good morning.' He says: 'I trust you are well?'

Oskar says: 'I am, Mr. Koch. How are you?'

Mr. Koch says: 'I can't complain.' He says: 'But come.' He waves with his hands towards the back of the truck. He says: 'These crates won't unload themselves.'

Isobel watches Oskar and Mr. Koch talk. She does not say anything.

Oskar and Mr. Koch go out into the alley.

Isobel follows them.

They go to Oskar's truck. Oskar gets into the back of the truck. Mr. Koch and Isobel stand outside the truck. Oskar hands a crate to Mr. Koch. He hands a crate to Isobel.

They go back into the store carrying the crates. Oskar follows them. He is also carrying a crate.

They put the crates they are carrying down by the door. They go back out into the alley and Oskar gets into the back of the truck. He hands a crate to Mr. Koch. He hands a crate to Isobel.

They go back into the store carrying the crates. They put the crates by the door. Mr. Koch stops. He leans against the pile of crates. He takes a handkerchief out of his pocket. He wipes his face with it.

Mr. Koch says: 'I am not as young as I used to be.'

Oskar smiles at Mr. Koch. He says: 'There aren't that many crates left.'

Isobel does not say anything. She can carry the crates now. It is not as hard as it was. She is stronger.

They go back out into the alley. They get more crates from Oskar's truck. They bring the crates into the store. They do this until there are no more crates in the back of Oskar's truck.

When there are no more crates Oskar closes the back of the truck. He takes off his work gloves. He turns to Mr. Koch.

Oskar says: 'Goodbye, Mr. Koch.'

Mr. Koch says: 'Goodbye, Oskar.' He says: 'I will see you tomorrow.'

Oskar says: 'Goodbye, Isobel.'

Isobel says: 'Goodbye, Oskar.'

Oskar turns to get into the truck. He does not get into the truck. He turns around again.

Oskar says: 'Isobel.' He says: 'I'm meeting some friends at the pub tonight.' He stops. He puts his hands in his pockets. He says: 'Would you like to come?'

Isobel shakes her head. She says: 'No.' She says: 'But thank you.'

Oskar shrugs his shoulders. He smiles to Isobel. He says: 'I'll see you tomorrow.'

He gets into his truck. He drives away.

Isobel goes back into the grocery store. Mr. Koch is already there.

Mr. Koch says: 'Well.' He wipes his face with his handkerchief. He puts his handkerchief back into his pocket. He says: 'Shall we get to work?'

Isobel nods her head.

Mr. Koch goes into his office. Isobel goes to the crates stacked next to the door.

She opens the crate on the top of the stack. There are cabbages inside the crate. She takes some of the cabbages out of the crate. She does not take all of them because there are too many for her to carry.

She takes them over to the cart by the door.

She puts the cabbages on the cart. She has to be careful that none of them fall off. She goes back to where the crate is. She takes more cabbages out of the crate. She takes them over to the cart.

She puts them on the cart. When she puts them on the cart the cart is full.

Isobel pushes the cart into the front of the store. She pushes it slowly. She does not want any of the cabbages to fall off the cart.

She goes into the store. There are rows of shelves in the front of the store. She pushes the cart past the shelves.

Isobel stops the cart.

She is in the front of the store. The produce is put out at the front of the store. She puts the cabbages on the cart onto a pile of cabbages.

There is a girl standing behind the cash register. She pretends she does not see Isobel. She is reading a magazine.

Isobel puts the cabbages on the cart with the cabbages that are already there. The cart is empty. She pushes the cart towards the back of the store.

She goes into the room at the back of the store. She leaves the cart by the door. She goes to where the crates are.

She hears Mr. Koch talking on the phone. He is in his office. He says: 'Madame, it is not for me to decide what she does.' He pauses. He listens. He says: 'Are you asking me to turn her out?'

Isobel stands in front of the crates. She listens to Mr. Koch.

Mr. Koch says: 'Goodbye, madame.' He puts the phone down. He puts it down too hard.

Isobel flinches.

Mr. Koch comes out of his office. Isobel is standing in front of the crates.

Isobel says: 'I'm sorry.'

Mr. Koch does not say anything. His face is red.

Mr. Koch opens the door to the alley. He pushes too hard on it. It bangs against the handrail on the steps outside. He goes outside. He stands at the top of the steps.

Isobel watches him take his cigarettes out of his waistcoat. He fumbles with them. He puts a cigarette to his mouth. He lights it.

He looks out into the alley. He smokes his cigarette.

Isobel stands in front of the crates beside the door. Mr. Koch is not looking at her. She does not know what she should do.

Mr. Koch smokes his cigarette. He puts it to his mouth and then he blows smoke out of his mouth.

Mr. Koch says: 'Isobel.' He is looking back into the store now. He is looking at Isobel.

He says: 'This is a simple place.' He puts his cigarette to his mouth. He says: 'And I am a simple man. I am at home here.'

He puts his cigarette to his mouth. He draws on it.

He says: 'But you, you are not so simple anymore.'

Isobel looks into the crate in front of her. She does not want to look at Mr. Koch. She pushes her hair so that it is not in her face.

She does not say anything. She cannot think of anything to say.

She nods her head.

She goes back to work. She opens the crate on the top of the pile. There are more cabbages inside it. She takes the cabbages out of the crate. She goes over to the cart. She drops one of the cabbages on the floor. Her hands are shaking. She picks it up.

She puts the cabbages on the cart.

Mr. Koch shakes his head. He finishes his cigarette. He goes back into his office. He starts his coffee-making machine.

Isobel opens another crate. There are tins in this crate. There is room on the cart for a few tins. She takes the tins out of the crate and puts them on the cart.

The cart is full. She takes the cart to the front of the store. She puts the things on the cart onto the shelves. The girl behind the cash register looks at her while she does. They do not speak to each other.

When the cart is empty she goes into the back of the store.

There are more crates in the back of the store. They have more things in them. She puts them out in the front of the store.

When all of the crates are empty she goes up to her room. She goes up the stairs. She closes the door behind her.

It is the end of the day. Mr. Koch is closing the store.

He locks the front door. He goes into the room in the back of the store. He stands at the bottom of the stairs.

Mr. Koch says: 'Isobel.'

He says: 'I am leaving now.' He says: 'Do you need anything for the night?'

Isobel says: 'No.'

She says: 'I will see you in the morning.'

Mr. Koch pauses a moment. He says: 'Well.' He is quiet a moment. He says: 'Have a good night, then.'

Isobel is in her room. She is sitting on the floor. Her notebook is on the floor in front of her.

Mr. Koch leaves the store. He locks the door when he leaves.

Isobel is sitting on the floor. She has her notebook open in her lap. She is writing.

It gets dark outside. She stands up. She goes to the middle of the room. She pulls on the cord hanging from the ceiling. The light turns on.

She looks at her room in the light. There is the sink on the wall and the mirror above it. There is the bed. There are plain white sheets on the bed. They are the way they have always been.

The room is different.

There is the towel hanging by the sink. There are clothes piled by the door. Isobel bought new clothes with the money Mr. Koch paid her.

Isobel goes back to where she was sitting. She sits down. She picks up the pencil she was using.

She writes.

She writes until she is finished the letter. She tears that page out of the notebook. She folds it. She puts it into an envelope. It is like the envelopes under the bed.

She holds the envelope with the letter inside it for a moment. She knows that she could send it. She seals the envelope. She puts it with the pile of envelopes under the bed.

It is late.

Isobel stands up. She is in her room. She does not want to be in her room.

She could leave her room. She could go down the stairs and out into the alley. It is not that late. She could go out. She could do something.

She puts on her sweater. She does up the buttons. She goes down the stairs. She goes out into the alley.

She takes her cigarettes out. She puts a cigarette between her lips. She lights it.

She draws on it.

It is colder out. Isobel wishes she were wearing gloves. She is not wearing gloves.

She exhales.

Isobel sits down on the steps. She smokes her cigarette.

When her cigarette is done she goes back into the store. She goes up the stairs. She goes into her room. She closes the door behind her. She takes off her sweater. She puts it on the floor.

She is tired. She does not know what time it is. She does not want to know what time it is.

She does not want to go to bed.

She looks at her bed. She sits on her bed. She puts her hands to her face.

She takes off her dress. It is not the dress she was wearing when she went to the train station. It is a new dress. It is plain and grey. It is good for working in. She is wearing stockings under it. They are warm. She takes them off. She puts them on the floor.

She sits on the bed in her underwear.

It is cold in the room. There are goosebumps on Isobel's skin.

She stands up. She turns off the light. She goes to the bed. She pulls the blankets back.

She stands beside the bed.

There is light from the alley coming in through the window. She looks out the window. There is nothing to see on the other side of the window.

She shivers. She is cold. She gets into the bed.

She lies on her back. She is looking at the ceiling.

She is not asleep.

She looks at the window. She cannot see out the window from where she is lying.

She does not move. She closes her eyes.

The letters she wrote are all under the bed. They are in envelopes. They are ready to be sent. She is not going to send them. She does not understand why but she is sure that she is not going to send them.

She rolls over onto her side. She curls her legs up against her body.

She is not asleep. She is not going to fall asleep. She will lie in bed awake. She does not know what else to do with herself.

She holds the blanket close to her body.

I don't remember you anymore. Sometimes I think that I do. But it's not real anymore, it's something that I've made up. It's not you.

What I have is a cigarette butt. There is nothing special about it. It's just a cigarette butt. I want it to be more than that. I need it to be more. I need it to mean something and I don't understand why it doesn't.

What do I do, Emile? How do I make it mean something?

When you sit down with a bunch of wood and some string, what do you do? How do you make something out of that?

It's late. The store is closed and I am in my room. I am sitting on my bed. I am too tired to say it's yours. I feel like giving up. I don't want to give up, Emile. I don't want to go home. I will not be sorry for what we did. I want us to mean something.

I am so tired and I have to be up early. I wish I didn't. I wish I wasn't here but I am. I can feel myself getting used to it. I am becoming the girl who lives in the room over the grocery store.

I hate it. I hate it for being so easy to get used to. I don't know what to do. I want there to be more than this but I don't know how to make something more than this.

I love you, Emile. I am trying to love you.

Emile is standing in front of a door. It is between two shops. On one side of it is a shop that sells magazines. On the other side is a tailor's shop. The shop that sells magazines is still open. There is someone inside it. She is looking at magazines.

There is a doorbell beside the door. Emile presses it.

From the other side of the door there is the sound of someone walking down stairs. Emile fidgets with his cap.

The door opens. Agatha is in the doorway.

She says: 'Hello, Emile.'

She leans forward so Emile can kiss her on the cheek. Emile kisses her on the cheek. She says: 'It's so good to see you.'

Emile smiles. He is carrying a reel of film. He has been to the shop where Agatha takes film to be developed. He spoke to the man who works there. The man wore thick glasses and his hair was starting to thin. He gave Emile the reel of film. Emile gave the man some money. He left. He came to Agatha's apartment.

Agatha says: 'Come in.'

She takes Emile's hand. She goes up the stairs. Emile follows her. At the top of the stairs there is another door. She opens it. She leads him through the door.

They are in Agatha's apartment. It smells of cigarettes and Agatha's perfume. There is a film projector set up in Agatha's living room. It is pointed at a wall. There is a sofa in front of it.

Emile gives Agatha the reel of film. She goes over to the film projector. She threads the film through the projector.

She says: 'Close the drapes, darling.'

Emile goes over to the window. He closes the drapes. It makes it dark in the room.

Agatha says: 'It'll be ready in a moment.' She is still threading the film through the projector. She points to the sofa. She says: 'Sit down. Pour yourself a drink.'

Emile sits on the sofa. It is a good sofa. There is a pattern embroidered on it. The pattern is of flowers and leaves.

There is a small table in front of the sofa. There are a bottle and two glasses on the table. Emile does not recognize the bottle. He picks the bottle up. He reads what is printed on the label. He still does not know what it is.

He pours some of what is in the bottle into the glasses. He smells it. It is strong.

Agatha says: 'There.'

She pushes a button. The projector turns on.

She sits down on the sofa. She picks up one of the glasses. She says: 'Cheers.' She touches her glass to Emile's.

She drinks from her glass. Emile sips from his. The projector clatters and throws light on the wall. Agatha settles into the sofa.

She touches Emile's arm. She says: 'I'm excited to see this.'

There is a room.

There is nothing moving in the room. There are two puppets here. They are standing close to each other. The suitcase that one of them was in is next to them. She has just stepped out of it.

She is standing next to the other one. He said things and now they are not saying things. He is holding her hand. She is resting her head on his chest.

It is quiet. They are not moving. They are waiting for what happens next.

The light in the room is dim. It keeps flickering. It is hard to see what is in the room. They are standing on a carpet. It is in the middle of the room. There is a bed against one wall and a dresser against another. The dresser is old.

Everything is old and falling apart.

He takes a step away from her.

Her head stays where it was when it was resting on his chest. She did not want him to step away. He lets go of her hand. It falls to her side.

He takes another step away from her.

It is what has to happen next. She does not try to stop him. She knows that it is what has to happen next.

He takes another step.

He is wearing a pair of boots and a jacket. The boots are heavy. He moves like he is not used to their weight.

She stands where she is. Where they were. She watches him moving away from her. She has not moved. She is watching him.

It is like she is figuring out what he is doing.

Her hands are touching in front of her body. She is not standing as straight as she could be. It is like she is nervous. But she watches him.

He is wearing a pair of boots and a jacket. The jacket is tattered. There is a patch sewn onto the back of it. It is covering a hole. There is a suitcase beside him. It is not the suitcase she was inside. It is small enough for him to pick up.

He bends down. He picks up the suitcase.

The light is dim. It flickers on and off. It is on top of the dresser and there is a lampshade over it. It is heavy with lace and trim. And dust. The room is heavy with dust. The light does not fill it. There is dust and darkness in all the corners.

He has the suitcase in his hand.

He walks away.

She cannot quite see him anymore. It is too dark. She does not look troubled that she cannot quite see him.

She stands with her hands held in front of her. She watches him.

The light flickers. It is dark. He keeps walking.

He is gone.

She cannot see him anymore. She can hear him walking. She does not know where he is. She does not know where he is going. All she can hear is the sound his boots make when he walks.

She turns her head away from the sound. Her shoulders slump and her whole body starts to sink. Her head starts to drop. She does not let her head drop. She raises it. She uses her hands to move the hair out of her face.

She stands straight.

She takes a step. She takes another step. She starts to walk.

She cannot hear him walking anymore. She hears a streetcar come. It does not stop. The sound of it rises and then falls away. There are things in the dark. Beyond the dresser and the bed and the lamp.

She goes towards them.

She is at the window. She moves the curtains aside.

There are lights on in the street outside. There are always lights on in the streets. They flicker in the dark. The city does not ever stop. She can see the streetcar moving away from her.

She puts her hands to the window. There is no one on the streetcar. There is no one out on the street.

She looks. There is nothing to see.

In the room there is a bed and there is a dresser. There is a suitcase open in the middle of the room. She feels around the edges of the window. She is looking for the latch. She opens the latch.

She pushes against the glass. The window opens.

She puts her hands on the window ledge. She steps through the window with one leg and then the other leg. She is hanging on to the window ledge with her hands.

A breeze lifts her dress up. The wind is cold against her legs.

She lowers herself into it.

She does not look back.

She lets go of the window. She falls to the ground. It is quiet. Then there is the sound of her taking a step, and then another step.

She is walking away.

Another streetcar goes by. It rings its bell as it goes through the intersection.

She is gone.

She is gone and everything goes black.

The film ends.

Agatha and Emile are sitting on her sofa. There is a table in front of the sofa. There is a bottle on it. Beside the bottle there are two glasses.

Agatha leans forward. She takes one of the glasses from the table. She drinks from the glass. She swallows. Emile can see her throat move when she swallows.

She puts her hand to her hair. Her hair is piled on top of her head. She checks to make sure it is still piled on top of her head.

She puts her glass back down on the table. She looks at Emile. She smiles. It is not a wolfish smile. There is something sad in her eyes. She says: 'Oh, Emile.'

She is not sure what else to say.

She stands up. She sways for a moment.

The projector is still running. Agatha walks over to the projector. She turns it off.

It clatters and then it stops. The room is dark. Emile takes the other glass from the table. He sips from it.

Agatha says: 'That was fantastic.'

She walks from the projector to the sofa. She is drunk. She is not moving steadily.

There is a lamp beside the sofa. Agatha turns the lamp on. She sits down beside Emile.

She does not say anything. She smiles. Her glass is on the table. She picks it up. She touches her glass to Emile's.

Her smile is wolfish again.

She says: 'Let me show it to some friends of mine.'

Emile drinks from his glass. He does not know what they are drinking. He is not sure that he likes it. He does not feel well. Agatha touches his arm.

She says: 'You wouldn't mind, would you?'

Emile shakes his head. He says: 'It is okay.'

Agatha drinks from her glass again. Emile does not drink from his glass.

She tips her head back. She empties her glass into her mouth. She licks her lips. Emile is sitting beside her on the sofa. He is holding on to his glass with both hands.

She reaches for the bottle. She pours some of what is in it into her glass.

She says: 'Emile. Give me your glass.'

Emile gives her his glass. She pours some of what is in the bottle into Emile's glass.

She puts the bottle back on the table. The bottle is almost empty. It was not almost empty when Emile arrived.

She picks up her glass with one hand. She picks up Emile's glass with her other hand.

She moves closer to Emile. She gives Emile his glass. Her skirt rides up on her legs.

She looks Emile in the eye. She touches Emile's glass with hers. She brings her glass to her mouth.

She drinks. She is looking at Emile. She is drunk. Her eyes are heavy.

Emile looks at his glass. He ducks his head down. He is breathing too fast. He does not like what they are drinking. He drinks from his glass.

Agatha touches his leg with her hand.

Agatha puts her glass on the table. She stands up. Standing up makes her dizzy. She rests her head in her hands until she feels less dizzy.

She straightens her skirt. She goes into her bedroom.

She comes out of her bedroom carrying a blanket. She puts it over Emile. He is lying crumpled on the sofa.

She bends over him. She touches his face with her hand. She says: 'Good night, Emile.'

He moves slightly. He settles under the blanket.

Agatha smiles. It is not a wolfish smile.

She kisses his cheek.

She picks his glass up off the floor. She puts it on the table. She turns out the light.

She goes back to her bedroom. She goes inside. She closes the door behind her.

Emile,

I went back to the train station. I went inside. I bought a ticket.

I spoke to the same woman who was there the day you left. She was still knitting that sweater. She stopped knitting to sell me a ticket and then she picked up her knitting again.

She didn't recognize me. I wanted her to recognize me. I wanted her to know what this meant. But I was just a girl to her.

I don't want to be just a girl.

I went out onto the platform. I had the cigarette butt from when you left. I put it back where I found it. It is just a cigarette butt. It can't be anything more than that.

I have nothing now, Emile. I don't know what will happen next. I don't know what I will do.

I am leaving.

I will not be the girl who lives over the grocery store. Not anymore. I don't know what I will be. I don't know and I am smiling.

I love you, Emile.

～ 12 ～

Isobel wakes up.

She is in her bed. She is lying between the sheets. It is light out. It is morning. There is light coming in through the window. It is not very much light. It is too early in the morning for there to be very much light.

There are specks of dust floating in the light.

Isobel sits up in bed. She pulls at her hair. She pulls at her hair and then she pulls it behind her head. She ties it into a knot so that it stays at the back of her head.

She gets out of bed. She goes over to the sink. She runs water into the sink.

She is standing in front of the sink. She is waiting for the sink to fill. There is a mirror over the sink. She can see herself in the mirror.

She looks at herself.

She is tall. She has dark hair and dark eyes. She is thin. She is not as thin as she was. She is stronger now. Her eyes are harder.

There is a washcloth beside the sink. She uses it to wash her face. She takes her underwear off. She uses the washcloth to wash the rest of her body.

When she is done she dries herself with the towel hanging next to the sink.

She goes to where her dress is lying on the floor. She picks it up. She puts it on. It is plain and grey. It is good for working in.

There is a suitcase by the door. There are other clothes inside it. They are new. Isobel bought them.

She goes past the suitcase. She leaves the room. She goes down the stairs. She is in the room at the back of the grocery store.

Mr. Koch is not here yet. He will be here soon but he is not here yet. It is still too early.

Isobel goes out into the alley. She is at the top of the steps that go down into the alley. She props the door open with the brick that Mr. Koch leaves beside the door.

Isobel is carrying a pack of cigarettes. It is in her hand. She takes a cigarette out of the pack. She puts it between her lips. She lights it with a match.

She draws on the cigarette.

She exhales.

She sits down on the top step. She holds her cigarette in her hand.

She waits.

She sits on the top step. She draws on her cigarette. She exhales. It is early in the morning. The light is sharp the way that it sometimes is this early in the morning.

She finishes her cigarette. She takes another one out. She puts it between her lips. She lights it.

Isobel hears the front door of the shop open. Mr. Koch is here. She does not turn around.

Mr. Koch walks through the grocery store. He came in the front door. He is walking through the store to the back.

He comes out the back door. He sees Isobel sitting at the top of the steps.

Mr. Koch says: 'Good morning, Isobel.'

Isobel says: 'Good morning, Mr. Koch.'

Mr. Koch goes back into the store. He goes into his office. He takes off his hat and his scarf and his overcoat. He starts his coffee-making machine.

He hums a tune to himself. It is the tune that he hums to himself every morning.

The coffee-making machine finishes making the coffee. Mr. Koch goes out to where Isobel is sitting. He is carrying two cups of coffee.

Isobel is sitting on the steps.

She is still smoking her cigarette. She smokes and she looks down the alley.

Mr. Koch chuckles. He says: 'Waiting for him will not make him come faster.'

He hands a cup of coffee to Isobel.

Isobel looks up at Mr. Koch. She smiles. She takes the cup of coffee.

Mr. Koch stands behind her. He reaches into one of the pockets of his waistcoat. He takes out a pack of cigarettes.

He puts a cigarette to his mouth. He takes a lighter out of another pocket of his waistcoat.

He lights the cigarette. He draws deeply on it. He blows smoke out into the air.

He makes a contented sound. It comes from deep in his throat. He drinks from his cup of coffee. Isobel is still looking down the alley. Mr. Koch looks at Isobel, then he looks down the alley with her.

They are waiting for Oskar to come with his truck.

Mr. Koch says: 'Are you all ready?' He is still looking down the alley.

Isobel does not say anything. If she said something she would have to turn around. She is looking down the alley.

She nods her head.

Mr. Koch and Isobel drink from their cups of coffee. They do not say anything more.

Mr. Koch finishes his cigarette. He flicks the butt of it away.

Mr. Koch says: 'Well.'

He says: 'I had best get to work.'

He is holding his cup of coffee. He drinks from it one last time.

Mr. Koch says: 'Come get me when Oskar comes.'

Isobel nods her head again.

Mr. Koch goes back into the grocery store. He goes into his office.

Isobel is still sitting on the steps behind the store. She finishes her cigarette. She takes out another cigarette. She puts it between her lips. She lights it.

She waits for Oskar to come.

Oskar's truck turns into the alley.

Isobel is still sitting on the steps. She is holding her cup of coffee in one hand.

She puts her cup down on the step beside her. It is empty.

She stands up. She stretches her arms up over her head. Oskar sees her. He honks the horn on his truck.

He stops his truck. He stops it so that the back of it is beside the steps going up into the store. He turns the engine off.

He gets out of his truck. He is standing by the steps that go into the grocery store.

Isobel is waiting for him there.

Oskar says: 'Good morning, Isobel.'

Isobel says: 'Good morning, Oskar.'

Oskar opens the back of the truck. There are crates in the back of the truck.

Oskar gets into the back of the truck. He puts his work gloves on. Isobel goes into the back of the store.

She says: 'Mr. Koch!' Mr. Koch comes out of his office.

Mr. Koch says: 'Is he here?'

Isobel says: 'Yes.'

Mr Koch says: 'Good, good.'

Mr. Koch and Isobel go out into the alley. Oskar is in the back of the truck.

Oskar says: 'Good morning, Mr. Koch.'

Mr. Koch says: 'Good morning, Oskar.' He says: 'And how are you today?'

Oskar says: 'I am well.' He says: 'How are you?'

Mr. Koch says: 'I am well enough.' He says: 'Come, let us get to it.'

They go out of the store. They go to Oskar's truck. Oskar is in the back of the truck. He hands a crate to Mr. Koch. He hands a crate to Isobel.

Isobel and Mr. Koch go into the store carrying the crates. Oskar follows them. He is also carrying a crate.

They put the crates they are carrying by the door and then they go back out into the alley. Oskar gets into the back of the truck. He hands a crate to Mr. Koch and he hands a crate to Isobel.

They go back into the store carrying the crates. Oskar follows them. He is also carrying a crate.

They put the crates by the door. They go back out into the alley. They get more crates from Oskar's truck. They bring the crates into the store.

They do this until there are no more crates in the back of Oskar's truck.

When there are no more crates Oskar closes the back of the truck. He takes off his work gloves. He turns to Mr. Koch.

Oskar says: 'Goodbye, Mr. Koch.'

Mr. Koch says: 'Goodbye, Oskar.' He says: 'I will see you tomorrow.'

Oskar says: 'Goodbye, Isobel.'

Oskar turns to get into the truck.

Isobel says: 'Wait.'

Oskar stops. He does not get into the truck. He turns around. He looks at Isobel. He puts his hands in his pockets. He says: 'Yes?'

Isobel takes a breath. She says: 'Do you go past the station?'

Oskar shrugs. He says: 'I could.'

Isobel says: 'Could you take me there?'

Oskar says: 'Sure.'

Isobel says: 'Thank you.'

She says: 'I need to get my things.'

Oskar says: 'Sure.' He takes his hands out of his pockets. He gets into the truck. He does not start the engine.

Isobel goes into the store. She goes up the stairs. She goes into her room.

There is the suitcase by the door. Isobel's things are in it. She picks up the suitcase. She looks at the room.

There is a bed in the room. It has plain white sheets on it. There is a blanket over the plain white sheets. There is a sink on the wall. There is a mirror over the sink and there is a window over the bed.

She looks at the room for the last time. She closes the door. She goes back down the stairs. She goes out of the store and into the alley.

Oskar's truck is there. Oskar is waiting. Mr. Koch is standing beside the truck.

Isobel goes to Mr. Koch. She puts her arms around him.

Mr. Koch smiles. He pats Isobel on the back.

Isobel says: 'Thank you.'

Mr. Koch says: 'Hush.' He says: 'Off with you now.'

Isobel gets into Oskar's truck.

Oskar is already in the truck. He starts the engine. They drive down the alley and then they turn onto the street.

Oskar looks at Isobel. He says: 'Where are you going?'

Isobel says: 'It doesn't matter.'

She says: 'I'm going away.'

They are sitting.

They are sitting, the two of them, on a bench on the platform of a train station.

It is early in the morning. They are waiting for a train to come.

They had been eating snacks. They had bought the snacks inside the station. There is a machine inside the station. It sells snacks. They put money into the machine and it gave them snacks.

They are not eating snacks anymore. They have eaten them. They are holding the wrappers that their snacks were in.

They want to say something.

They do not. It is too quiet. They should say something. There is nothing left to say. There is only what is going to happen.

Instead of saying something they are holding the wrappers their snacks were in.

They are sitting on a bench on the platform of a train station. They are waiting for a train to come. It is why they are here. They know that it is why they are here. They do not need to say it. They know.

It is all that there is to say. There is no need to say it.

There is nothing to say.

She says: 'I don't want it to be like this.'

Her hands are in her lap. She is holding on to the wrapper from her snack. Her hands are twisting it. She watches her hands twist it.

He does not say anything.

She does not look at him. She looks at her hands. She looks at how the paper wrapper twists. She says: 'I don't want it to be like this.'

He says: 'What should we do?'

She says: 'I don't know.'

She stops speaking. She pulls on the piece of paper in her hands. She pulls it until it rips.

She says: 'I don't know.'

She says: 'I want to see you again.'

She looks at her hands. Her hands are holding the pieces of the paper her snack was wrapped in.

She says: 'Will I see you again?'

She still does not look at him. The paper wrapper in her hands is in three pieces. He looks at her hands. He does not touch her hands. He wants to but he does not.

He does not know what to do.

He looks at her.

He says: 'I do not know.'

He is quiet. He looks at his hands. He is holding a paper wrapper in his hands. He cannot see what is written on it clearly. His eyes are wet.

He says: 'I hope so.'

She looks at him. She says: 'Okay.'

She smiles.

They are sitting on a bench on the platform of a train station. They are sitting beside each other.

They are waiting for a train to come.

It is almost time for the train to come. They cannot see the train. They know that the train is close but they cannot see it yet.

She says: 'What will you do?'

He says: 'I will go home.'

He says: 'I will find Nicolas. I will find him and we will go home.' He says: 'I will meet Agatha.'

He says: 'I will give her the film.'

She says: 'And then?'

He says: 'Agatha will show the film.'

She says: 'And then?'

He says: 'I do not know.'

He is quiet for a moment.

He says: 'I will do something.' He says: 'I do not know what it will be.' He says: 'I will get caught up in something.'

He says: 'It is what happens there.'

The train has not come. They still cannot see it. It does not matter that they cannot see it. They know that it is coming.

They know what will happen.

They do not have to say anything. It will not change what will happen. They both know what will happen.

He says: 'What will you do?'

She says: 'I don't know.'

They are sitting on a bench. They are sitting beside each other. They are sitting close beside each other.

ACKNOWLEDGEMENTS

There are people I would like to thank for their support while I was writing this book: Bryony Henderson, Michelle Horacek, Barbara Bridger, Ted Blodgett, Katharine Southworth, Leigh Gillam, Emma Hooper, Jacob Wren, Olchar Lindsann, Sharon Budnarchuk, David McDerby, Barry Corber and, most of all, Carina de Klerk.

This book is dedicated to the memory of Gilbert Bouchard (1961–2009). I wish you could have seen this, old friend.

ABOUT THE AUTHOR

Alan Reed is the author of a collection of poems, *For Love of the City*. He lives in Montreal.

Typeset in Fournier
Printed and bound at the Coach House on bpNichol Lane

Edited and designed by Alana Wilcox
Cover puppet and photo by Leigh Gillam

Coach House Books
80 bpNichol Lane
Toronto ON M5S 3J4

416 979 2217
800 360 6360

mail@chbooks.com
www.chbooks.com